WINTER
GAMES

DANIEL CHURCH

NEW WAVE BOOKS

Published in 2022 by New Wave Books
Copyright © 2022 by Daniel Church

This novel's story and characters are fictitious.
Certain businesses, institutions, agencies,
and public offices are mentioned, but the
characters involved are wholly imaginary.

Cover photo by gadaian.

ISBN 978-1-7362680-0-1

In remembrance of the souls needlessly lost to cold.

I

The ice age is coming, the sun's zoomin' in
Meltdown expected, the wheat is growin' thin

—The Clash, "London Calling"
(Songwriters: Joe Strummer and Mick Jones)

1

As he usually did, Whit Thorgason had come to the Islands alone. Surfing the North Shore was something he treated himself to every couple of years, and it was an intense enough experience that having a friend along tended to be a distraction. He stretched his long limbs, alternately seated and standing on the beach, while he studied the hurtling, thundering sets of waves with sun-flecked hazel eyes. Fine mist raised by the surf shone in the morning sun and gave the beach and nearby ocean a honey-yellow hue; the sand shook beneath him. After he had sensed the swell's rhythm, he plunged into the foamy, churning water near shore with his board. The rip current sped him as he paddled to where surfers waited for waves in a loose cluster. In ten minutes, it was his turn. He paddled for a wave with a twenty-foot face; completing the initial, heart-pounding drop and two difficult inside sections made him feel that his day had started. After riding his second wave, he noticed a dreadlocked surfer, Micah Ritchie, whom Whit had seen in magazines in the past, paddling toward the lineup and looking a little disoriented. Ritchie was said to have cycled through friends and made more than one wrong choice since moving to the North Shore. Though Whit would have expected him to look at ease on a big day like this, he was staring straight ahead like people sometimes did when they had hypothermia. Whit knew it was a more common occurrence among surfers in the Islands than most non-surfers would typically believe.

"You good?" Whit asked him.

Ritchie, who gave off a tough-guy, druggy vibe, nevertheless saw that Whit's eyes showed good intentions and gave him a shaka sign in response. Although meant to reassure, the way he formed the sign and, even more so, the look in his brown eyes let Whit know that the disorientation was worse than he first thought. Ritchie, in turn, could see he hadn't managed to reassure Whit. No one out in serious waves likes anyone seeing them in a weakened state. He paddled far enough from Whit to make awkward further efforts at communicating with him.

They were at a part of the Sunset Beach break where it was easy to get in trouble when sets of big, fast waves came through without warning. Whit was good enough to be tolerated by the locals, even within this one stretch of water where people were more prone to get grumpy, but for now, his focus wasn't on avoiding pissing off locals; it was on saving one. His best hope was to break through the man's brain fog with odd behavior and impressive surfing.

He whistled to indicate a wave rearing up was his, jumping the line slightly. It was the kind of thing someone could pull once a year at most at a hotly contested break like this—if the person surfed the wave well, which Whit managed to do.

When he paddled back out, two or three locals whom he could expect to throw some shade his way didn't look at him twice; he stopped paddling and took a spot among the surfers eying the horizon and talking game ("still building"... "maxing later today"... "yesterday was sweet," and the like). Ritchie was one of them, looking worse by the minute. Whit paddled near him like they were surfing brothers from way back. "Dude,"

Whit said. "You've got hypothermia. You're going to need to paddle in."

"What, are you a doctor, brah?" Ritchie said.

"Not a doctor, but someone who has spent time on glaciers," Whit said. "I know it's awesome out here, but I've seen a guy die from this, and you look the way he did."

"Like, how?"

"Like, disoriented," Whit said. "Your lips are blue . . . goosebumps . . . shaking. I can see you trying to control it, but I can also see you can't."

"So, like, I'll have a tea when I'm done and get in the shower, brah," Ritchie said.

"That might not do it," Whit said, brushing his dripping brown hair away from his eyes. He looked around toward the other surfers to see if he might enlist help from anyone. What he mostly saw in their faces was faint annoyance that he was talking so much. "You've got to find a different way in; you're in no shape to surf right now," he said.

Ritchie looked at him, water dripping from the ends of his dreadlocks, his clenched jaw showing fear beneath layers of machismo and real courage that he had accumulated over a lifetime of surfing at spots like this.

"I'm not sure the best way, now that I think about it," Whit said. Ritchie's eyes showed alarm as he realized Whit was neither lying nor completely full of shit. "Maybe if I coach you through paddling for the smallest wave, you could drop to your stomach and bodyboard to shore?" It wasn't much of a plan, but it had good intentions behind it, and Ritchie, despite his brain fog, could feel that.

"Yeah, I think maybe," he said. The other surfers had caught wind of what was happening; a short-looking and tattooed

Asian guy paddled toward Whit, close enough to say quietly: "Should I maybe, like, take a wave to shore and call 911?"

"That would be good," Whit said.

"He was the last one out last night and the first one in this morning," the guy said. "It's, like, a thing with him."

Soon the volunteer had caught a wave and disappeared.

"Okay, you're next," Whit told Ritchie. "Can you make the wave and ride on your stomach?"

Things weren't trending positively; Ritchie's condition was worsening.

"I think I can," he said.

"This one," Whit said firmly, although with a tinge of embarrassment—he was talking to a man whose surfing was better than his own as though he were a ten-year-old boy.

"I see it," Ritchie said.

The wave was nearly on them; Ritchie spun his board, caught the wave, and disappeared. The back of the rushing wave was too high for Whit to see over; there was no way to know if Ritchie had succeeded. Whit turned to the horizon to catch and ride the next one. The others ceded position, understanding what he was doing. It was another hairy drop, but he made it. For the final third of the wave, he dropped to his stomach the same way he'd instructed Ritchie.

Nearing shore, he untethered his leash, walked onto the sand, and dropped his board. He sprinted to a circle of people surrounding Ritchie.

The circle opened to let him in. He registered that most of the people present were surfers, plus a handful of tourists, at least one of whom looked pretty upset. The circle parted again for two EMTs arriving. Whit recognized them as prominent surfers, as many lifeguards and EMTs were on the North Shore.

As they took up positions on either side of Ritchie, who had become unconscious, witnesses and pseudo-witnesses shouted out what they thought was going on:

"Bad wipeout."

"Drug overdose."

"He's just high."

"Drowned."

"Hit his head."

He wasn't surprised Ritchie had passed out. Whit figured his core temperature had gone down dangerously since he'd left the water. By this point, he had a few things working against him: wet surf trunks, hair, and skin, coupled with strong trade winds blowing; he no longer benefited from the warmth of shaking. Adrenaline was undoubtedly the only thing that had kept him conscious out in the water.

"Pretty sure he's hypothermic," Whit said, addressing himself to the EMTs. "He was shaking in the lineup but not now." The EMTs were running diagnostic tests. There were cases when it was the least of the problems facing a surfer pulled onto the beach like this; there were broken backs, concussions, drug overdoses, and strokes, to name a few. And many of the issues could be accompanied and worsened by hypothermia.

Whit knew the medics had to rule the other things out, but waiting was still hard. As they felt for a pulse, pulled back Ritchie's eyelids, took blood pressure, and looked for signs of trauma to his upper body and head, there were reasons for Whit to fear he was going to see a person die of hypothermia for the second time in his life. Still, the EMTs were good at their jobs, and hypothermia rarely progressed to death in such conditions. Four more EMTs ran toward them from the parking lot with a stretcher. The crowd parted a third time; the most

recently arrived EMTs placed the stretcher next to Ritchie's
pale form. After strapping him to it, they counted—"one, two,
three"—and lifted. The next thing Whit knew, he was jogging
next to the stretcher, instinct guiding him. "Are you riding with
me?" one of the EMTs asked.

"Yeah," Whit said. The ambulance doors swung shut, closing
in Ritchie, the EMT, and Whit. Moments later, the ambulance
careened from the parking lot and started north on the highway
toward the area's community hospital.

"Not his first ride in here," the EMT said.

"No?" Whit said. "Likes it somehow?"

"Ever had hypothermia?" the EMT asked.

"Nothing to talk about," Whit said. "A little, maybe."

"Enough to get euphoric?" the EMT said.

"A tiny bit," Whit said.

"Let's just say he seems to like that part of it," the EMT said.

"Do you have a way to warm a saline drip?" Whit asked.

"The hospital's three minutes away. They've got pre-warmed
drips."

Soon Whit felt a tiny jolt as the ambulance hit the lip of an
entrance; then, they were arcing to a stop in the curved driveway
in front of the Emergency Department. Whit followed as hospital staff pushed the gurney, running, through the entryway,
past a reception counter, and to a treatment room, where a doctor, nurses, and orderlies waited.

"You can't be in here, sorry," one of the orderlies said to Whit,
who found his way to the waiting room. Once he was ensconced
on a gold-vinyl couch, copies of *People*, *Good Housekeeping*, and
Sports Illustrated on the coffee table in front of him vied for his
attention. With no conscious intention guiding him, he took an
issue of *Good Housekeeping* in his hands, leaving its cover closed

out of a half-formed hope that the spirit of normalcy with which the people had put the magazine together would somehow turn this day around.

When he saw the doctor walking toward him just half an hour later, Whit was pretty sure that things had worked out from how the man's shoes hit the floor. He stood to receive the news, whatever it would be.

"He should be fine," the doctor, who was tan and fit and tall like Whit, said. "Even surfing for days on end the way you guys do shouldn't have done that to him, but hypothermia can be a little weird. From what I hear, you're a big reason he got here when he did, and that was a good thing."

"Thank you," Whit said.

"Thank you," said the doctor before rushing off, presumably to the next patient on his list.

To Whit's mild surprise, his board, with its leash neatly wrapped around the tail the way he would do himself, had been set above the high-water mark on the beach. He gratefully picked it up, noted no one in sight to whom to give thanks, and walked toward the parking lot. By this time, he had a chill himself after riding in the ambulance in a pair of wet board shorts and a wet rash guard and waiting in the air-conditioned hospital. Even if he hadn't been cold, he felt no pull to ride any more waves in his last hours in the Islands; he'd already experienced more than a full day's worth of life. Instead, he drove his rented SUV to his short-term apartment to start the process of returning to the mainland.

2

Although the day on which Ritchie had gotten hypothermia was early within the ascendancy of the Climatists when there were fewer reasons to question their premises, it made a big impression on Whit. It let him see more clearly the perils of cold, even though he thought he'd known them well, more so after Oliver Brown's hypothermic death years earlier.

Whit hadn't followed his parents' footsteps in glaciology to make them happy. And he also hadn't gone into it to live within a closed-off brotherhood of fellow scientists, leaving the public on the other side of high stone walls erected by jargon, the ability to do code, and esoteric knowledge concerning, among other things, the triple point of water.

It was, rather, that he loved it. It was his first romance, and it had never stopped making him feel fortunate. The math, the chemistry, the physics, the computer modeling, the geology, the hydrology—all the things on which glaciology drew—came easy. And true north—as he progressed from public school in Grand Rapids to finishing his PhD at the University of Oslo in three years rather than four—was a love of glaciers present in him before his parents explained essential features of the science to him. He loved the expanses of ice. Traveling with one of his parents, and sometimes with both, to glaciers in South America, Asia, the Arctic, and Europe, as well as to those in the Rockies and Cascades, he was fond of everything about them: the sounds the water made rushing across and under them; the feel of the air above them; the way sound carried across the ice; the way the glaciers and the mountains felt like a single entity, one inseparable into parts. He loved the animals on glaciers, including the diuca finch, which he admired for its ability to feed its young in an incredibly challenging environment.

As a star faculty member who attended several conferences a year on the university's tab (which was, in turn, on the government's tab), he occasionally managed a first-class upgrade, and that was what he did at the counter in Honolulu. He wasn't sure why anyone who had to pay out of their pocket would shell out three times the cost of an economy seat. However, as the plane descended into smog over Denver on this late-January day, he realized he had experienced nearly unbroken thought for seven straight hours, a nearly impossible feat in the economy cabin.

While the plane taxied, he took up the thoughts he had been spinning during the flight. He lived in a time when the public believed the earth was warmer than it had ever been (*it wasn't*), storms of all kinds were worse than they had ever been (*they weren't*), the wildfires CNN showed on television each summer burned more acres than ever before (*they didn't*). All of which led to something like generalized terror about global warming, climate change, global weirding, or the "climate crisis"—the most recent of the efforts to rebrand weather ignorance.

For reasons he only obscurely understood, he cared more that people underestimated the perils of cold (prominent among them hypothermia) than he did about their mistaking the glacial retreat of the past century and a half as proof of runaway global warming. Watching Micah Ritchie's fight with hypothermia, as his core temperature fell to the point of disorientation in a tropical paradise, brought the truth about the subject home for Whit on a new level.

He waited at the baggage carousel with a cart until his duffel bag came down the conveyor, went to the baggage office to retrieve his board bag containing his three surfboards, and pushed the cart topped by his beige, nine-foot-long bag out of the terminal to his red, surf-rack-topped Land Cruiser. Closing the rear gate, he realized, though only faintly, that the last twenty-four hours would be significant for him.

Driving through flurries to Boulder on a bitterly cold morning, he reflected on the misconceptions surrounding his field. Before arriving at college, he had known that glaciers advanced and retreated for dozens of reasons and that one of the least weighty among them was air temperature. He knew that humidity was a significant factor, as was the amount of wind crossing the ice. Insolation, the amount of sun hitting a given location, bore an enormous impact, too. At constant atmospheric temperature and increased insolation, a glacier could shrink. At *lower* temperatures and increased insolation, it would often *still* shrink. No one had measured humidity or insolation globally throughout the century and a half of global warming, which meant it was impossible to know if the whole system had gained heat or why a percentage of glaciers were advancing, others retreating, and some remaining stable.

Determining the dynamics of a single glacier was infinitely interesting, infinitely complex, and incomprehensible to the average climate protester who had never read an academic article in a largely uninformed, if well-intentioned, life. Indeed, it was maddening to Whit that people with no knowledge of his field, once they had heard what he did for a living, tossed off platitudes about the meltdown they believed they were seeing unfold. But the same people, believing themselves present at Armageddon, did not see the connection between society's terrified flight from fossil fuels to expensive, unreliable power sources and people dying in their homes from what had nearly killed Ritchie. You could call the new power sources "renewables"—or anything else—and they would have the same effect. The simple truth was that once you had made energy expensive enough to satisfy the Climatists, you had a subset of the global population who could no longer afford the cost of keeping their homes warm enough to survive. Retirees were especially likely to economize in the face of higher heating costs and die in the effort, but they were not the only ones.

The British government had been counting the unfortunate (tens of thousands) who died annually of cold-related illnesses—including influenza, pneumonia, and hypothermia—for decades, as had Canada. Inevitably, there were many whose silent departures escaped the notice of authorities. Whit knew that the people, counted or uncounted, discussed on the TV news or kept hidden, perished just the same in a hundred countries or more. If you could ever total them up globally, they would surely number in the hundreds of thousands every year.

It was this that ate at him.

"Flight okay?" Amy said, kissing him in their modest entryway. She was in her pajamas, which meant she was working. Her eyes were green with yellow flecks, and her shoulder-length hair was light brown.

"First-class upgrade," he said, in a near monotone.

"You seem stressed for a guy who just flew first class," Amy said.

"Yesterday affected me more than I might have mentioned," he said.

"You said the guy's going to be okay," Amy said.

"The doctor said he will be," Whit said, "but it's just weird how no one else was helping him, and weird it happened at all."

"Divers get hypothermia in warm places sometimes," she said. "It's not *that* weird."

"I went with him in the ambulance, mostly because no one else was volunteering to go with him, and it felt like there should be. Not like it mattered; he was unconscious."

"It was a good thing to do," Amy said.

"I'm like a walking hypothermia curse."

"He didn't die," she said.

"Unlike Oliver Brown," Whit said.

"Oliver Brown didn't die because of anything you did, or didn't, do," she said.

"Maybe," Whit said. "This still brought it back."

"I could see how it would," she said. "What was the surfer's name?"

"Micah Ritchie," Whit said. "Kind of a druggy dude, but crazy talented in the water."

"Are you going to reach out to him?" she asked.

"No," Whit said. "He only just barely let me help him when he needed it."

"Well, maybe he'll do something like you did for someone else down the line," she said.

"I like that idea," Whit said.

They made their way to the sofa in the living room, where they sat opposite each other, with their backs on the armrests.

Amy McPherson Thorgason, his "dramatically better half," as he referred to her, was a chemist who had sailed through her schooling much as he had. Her *published* dissertation garnered a post-doc position at the University of Colorado–Boulder a couple of buildings away from his. They had no doubt passed each other on the pathways connecting their buildings, but they met at a Halloween party for scientists. They had both come wearing pocket protectors as their only costumes and had ended up talking deep into the night.

The party seemed a decade past; in truth, it had only been four years. But they were significant: They married and bought a house.

She had an uneasy feeling as they sat in silence for a moment.

He told her a fuller version of the story, including how he'd found his surfboard.

"It's crazy," he said.

"What?" she said.

"I didn't know the guy, but it felt like someone important to me was in trouble."

"I think I get it," she said.

"No one on the beach knew what it meant," Whit said, closing his eyes.

"That you've got to be careful, even in the tropics, to maintain your body temperature?" Amy said.

"Yeah, that," he said, reopening his eyes. "But also, that, as a species, we're just so vulnerable to cold," Whit said. "Just like my parents said, cold is heartless and wants us dead."

"Well, it wasn't exactly *cold* that day, right?"

"It wasn't at all, but that's the point," he said. "It doesn't take much to kill a human being, just a little absence of warmth for a handful of hours in certain circumstances, and it can all be over."

"And?" Amy said.

"And it drives me nuts that people think the earth is too warm," he said.

"You've told me that once or twice," Amy said with a wry smile.

"He could have died," Whit said. "That's the point."

"I don't see it," Amy said. "Hypothermia's one thing; dying from it is something else."

"Yes and no," Whit said. "I'm pretty sure Micah Ritchie has some health issues, maybe from his lifestyle. And it didn't look good there for a while."

"But this had a *happy* ending, right?" Amy said.

"I guess," Whit said. "People don't know what kind of planet they live on. They don't."

3

It was chaos on the fourth floor of 30 Rockefeller Center. "Who's seen the video?" Erica Nagle said. A Syracuse grad, she was a lifelong New Yorker with beautiful daughters, eight and four, who looked a lot like her. There was also a husband with a big-time career and a trustworthy nanny whom she feared ever losing.

"Chip has seen it," Ben Rogers said. He had come to NBC from an affiliate in the South after a strong series of reports on corrupt officials at a hospital chain. Balding but handsome, with twinkling gray eyes, he graduated near the top of his class at Auburn and was on his second wife, with whom he had a young son.

"Just Chip?" Erica said.

"Chip, Walter, Jessica, Brad, and maybe some others," Ben said.

"But not you."

"I object to it, on principle," he said.

They sat next to each other in the 10 A.M. production meeting for *NBC Nightly News.* The video had come in overnight; it was shocking that it had not been shown on air already, at least in part. Meanwhile, it was a minor miracle that their show still existed in 2028. Online news had advanced to where those who wanted to know what was happening at a given moment could. Where in-the-field reporting had long been the standard process for the three networks' competing national news shows, now it was a rarity, with glorified video curating replacing it as the mainstay. The footage came in, and telegenic studio "reporters" contextualized it with just enough of the seeming transparency from the days of yore to induce a couple of million people to tune in. The jobs that Ben and Erica and everyone else in the conference room had were coveted and permanent—if you performed.

There were executives from upstairs standing around the periphery of the room. Erica and Ben had yet to see many of them before, though they had both been with the network for years.

Charles "Chip" Sutcliffe stood at the head of the table, behind a chair where he would usually sit. No one had seen him do this before, though Sutcliffe always had another gear, no matter the situation.

"This is not a good thing," he began, creating silence in the room without having to ask for it. A fierce squash player, poet, and handsome man for someone pushing sixty with an acne-scarred face, Sutcliffe had handled any number of crises within *The Nightly News*, and within the nation, during his nearly two decades running the show. He pushed a long lock of still-brown hair away from his forehead. "It's not a good thing for us . . . or for anyone." The silence in the room held.

"We will watch this, and no one will say anything about it. Not for a few minutes. We have a situation, and I'm going to need people's best thoughts on the table, okay?" Staffers expressed understanding with faint nods and shrugs of their shoulders. Sutcliffe didn't usually talk this way, and if he was doing so now, there must have been a reason. "Matthew," Sut-cliffe said to a tech.

The lights dimmed, and navy curtains silently parted to reveal a large-screen TV on the other side of the room from where Sutcliffe stood; on the screen, which was frozen on a paused video, there was a scientific laboratory in which a nerdy-looking guy in glasses looked into the camera. Something about how he held his eyes made it seem to more than one in the room that he was looking right at *them*. It almost seemed as if he could see you, as crazy as that was. He wore short pants, flip-flops, and a red-on-white Spiderman T-shirt. He looked to be in his fifties and was fit and tan. He was seated on a metal folding chair with three box fans pointed at him.

"Here we go," Sutcliffe said. "Matthew?" The tech un-paused the video with a remote, and the man on the screen began to speak.

"My name is Michael O'Brien. I am a tenured faculty member at the University of Wyoming in the Department of Geology and Geophysics. The time-temperature stamp you see in the upper right corner of the screen will give context to the events being recorded. Please note that the ambient temperature in the lab is fifty-nine degrees Fahrenheit. This is the global mean temperature, referred to by news organizations and many of my fellow scientists as 'unprecedentedly hot.' The fans here are set on low to create as nearly as possible a typical wind speed in Earth's temperate zone, approximately seven miles an hour."

Erica, Ben, Sutcliffe, the rest of the producers, and all the executives watched the screen with rapt attention; it was as though time stood still.

"It is not knowable how long this will take. The equipment will record for ten seconds starting at the top of every third hour; when my fitness watch"—here O'Brien flashed a watch to the camera—"shows a pulse of zero, the video will be auto-zipped and distributed to a list I have created over the past few weeks. If you are among the first to watch this and are seeing it somewhere other than your home or on a device you own personally, then you are either on that list or share an employer with someone on the list.

"I am not happy to be bringing my life, which has been beautiful and satisfying, to a premature end. However, I will not stand by as science gets hijacked, from without and from within, by people who should know better, with the result that human living conditions have plummeted in a half-generation, and children throughout the industrialized world believe they are living in end times.

"I won't be a party to that. And I won't abet it. I love the world, its people, and science too much to let that process unfold without a fight.

"Don't fear what you are about to see; there will be no violence."

When O'Brien had finished his introduction, the time stamp jumped to 03:00:00, and his body temperature—previously 98.5 degrees Fahrenheit—stood at 96.9 degrees. Next to it on the screen, there was his pulse: 117.

"As you can see, my arms and legs are covered with goosebumps, and I am shivering."

The next time-temperature stamp showed 06:00:00, and a few people around the room gasped as the video started to advance. After being in average conditions on the planet for such a short time, O'Brien's temperature had fallen to 95.1 degrees, and his heart rate, striving to keep him warm, had risen to 119. That was hard to take in, but what was far harder was O'Brien's evident mental state. From the upbeat aspect that his face held three hours before, he now looked befuddled. He had a tick in his right eye, another in his neck. The stress of trying to think clearly in his condition made him look confused, trending toward psychotic. His hands held the metal seat of the chair as he fought the instinctual urge to get up and do jumping jacks, run around the lab, or do anything to raise his pulse and save his life.

"This is more uncomfortable than I thought," he said. "I remember I'm doing something good, and I'm not going to waver. But I can't stop thinking of the wood stove in my favorite cabin."

Though Erica and the others could make out the words, his speech was slurred; he was obviously in dire trouble already.

During the hour-nine check-in, O'Brien's eyes were closed, and he was still holding onto the chair with both hands. His temperature was 91 degrees; his pulse was 102.

At the twelve-hour check-in, O'Brien lay in a heap before the folding chair. The thermometer indicated 90; the heart-rate monitor showed 63. His body's fight to regulate his temperature had largely ended.

At fifteen hours, the scene was as it had been three hours earlier, to the extent that O'Brien's body hadn't moved. The thermometer had fallen to 85; the heart-rate monitor had descended to 48. People in the conference room watching the video were motionless, barely blinking.

At eighteen hours, nothing had changed, but the thermometer showed 71; the heart-rate monitor, 0.

The tech turned the screen to black and pushed the button that closed the curtains.

Even if Sutcliffe hadn't required silence from those assembled for the first minutes after the video, the people assembled in the room likely would have given it to him. Those seated looked at the table; the ones standing looked at the curtains covering the television screen or at their own feet. Amazingly, only one person looked at a phone. It was the first suicide any of them had witnessed; nearly all were perplexed by what, beyond that, Sutcliffe, who had seen the video previously, expected of them.

"We can't run it," Erica said.

"Right, but why?" Sutcliffe said. "This will end up being news, and people will wonder why we didn't cover it."

"Well, there's right, and there's wrong," Erica said. She had made two trips to Greenland with production teams since coming to the show in 2021, and each trip had yielded proof that water runs off glaciers and that this scares people watching it on TV. Ratings had been high; for the three-part series based on the second trip, Emmys had come in. "It doesn't matter that you can die in fifty-nine-degree temperatures. It's a false experiment, and it will make people think climate change isn't real. That man was wrong to kill himself, and we'd be wrong to show him on TV."

The only person in the room who had shown the pluck to keep her phone out throughout the last twenty minutes was Veronica Johnson. With dishwater-blond hair in a bun and all but no makeup to hide her distractingly glamorous good looks, she was an occasional on-air reporter who had a strong career as a producer before that; she raised her hand as if to ask a question.

"Chip?" she said.

"Yes?"

"It's on CNN. The chyron says: 'Climate denier takes life with hypothermia chamber.' They decided for us, I'd say."

"Wrong is wrong," Erica said.

"Most news is wrong," Johnson said, "if you're going to go there."

"Most news is not wrong," Sutcliffe said, rapping the table with his fingertips with enough force to turn heads.

"I didn't mean inaccurate," Johnson said.

"I know what you meant," Sutcliffe said.

Ben decided to chip in.

"Well, fortunately or unfortunately, this is going to be old when we put it on," he said. "At this point, the game becomes who can learn the most about O'Brien and show him as the whack job he clearly was the most successfully."

Looking up from the table to the corporate visitors long enough to give the respectful, if fleeting sense that he required their assent, Sutcliffe said only: "Get on it."

The room cleared. Walking through the double doors propped open by the tech and a production assistant, all who had been present were clear about one thing: The gears of history, generally silent, or nearly so, had just ground loudly enough to be heard.

4

There was, for a long time, a temptation to believe that the purveyors of English-language news had found their way to the center of the universe. Production values were high; the on-air talent was whip-smart; writing was first-rate; and the history of presidents toppled, corporate conspiracies exposed, and criminals brought to justice was glorious. If you watched a lot of the product, and everyone who mattered did, it seemed almost as if you were bearing witness to the mind of God. Faintly, there was a glimmer of an understanding that other perspectives, other news productions, and other realities existed in the world; but it required effort to keep this fact in mind. In the face of the torrent of news emerging from one's television screen, even clever people forgot all the time: Not everyone spoke English; not everyone saw the world in remotely similar ways to, for instance, Americans.

In 2028, one person who saw things differently than most citizens of the United States was Juanita Tagawa of Chile. Her experience of Michael O'Brien's last moments was in a bar in Concepción. She had managed for a long time running not to have a television in her apartment. As an artist, she had learned that the amount of work she got done each week fell with a television in her living space. But two or three nights a month, more if world happenings took a worrying turn, she came to La Paz, the most civilized bar she knew, to watch the day's events and have a glass of wine. Poster-sized photos of Spanish-speaking Nobel peace and literature prize laureates adorned the walls, a play on the establishment's name. A second draw for her was that in a world gone mad, La Paz was a place where people never argued. The owner, Marguerite, was the daughter of a diplomat; she had witnessed too many self-important fools sparring in other watering holes and cafés around town to permit hot-headed verbal disputes in her own. For those who knew, La Paz was worth the extra money drinks cost for the quality of thinking one could do within its walls.

On the night news of the strange suicide broke, Juanita, a typically modern Chilean of mixed Mapuche, Spanish, and Japanese heritage, didn't hear the newscaster's lead-in. However, when she looked up, she saw the same thing the *Nightly News* staff had seen on the screen in their conference room: the lab, the guy with the Spider-Man T-shirt, in this case with subtitles on the screen, and a chyron reading: "American scientist kills himself with cold."

It was too weird, too far away, and too poorly contextualized for anyone in the bar to make anything of it. It was vaguely satisfying, for some, just to read the words "American scientist kills himself," but that was the extent of the effect of Michael O'Brien's last act on all the habitués of La Paz—except one.

"*Miguel*," Juanita said. She watched him on his chair, speaking in his recognizably erudite way, then looking suddenly ill, then lying in a heap on the floor. She observed his spiking, then declining, then stilled pulse.

Juanita goodbye-kissed Maria on both cheeks (saying, "I'll explain"), paid her tab, and walked out the door. Michael had come to Concepción when they were both younger and at the front end of their careers. He was a geologist who loved a surf break just south of town, one that tourists typically skipped. She used to paint on the beach when she wasn't surfing herself. When Michael happened upon her easel and saw someone who looked like him pictured surfing on it, he pointed and asked if it was him: "*So yo?*" She gave him a gruff nod of the chin, disappointed in herself that she had accidentally painted a gringo. "*Tu me pagas?*" Michael dared to ask, asking if she planned to pay him. Her face was beautiful, with eye-catching features coming down to her on both sides of the family; dark-brown eyes, light-brown skin, and high cheekbones complemented one another. But her greatest attractions were her centered confidence and creative spark. Rather than from her DNA, these had been fought for and gave her the presence of an older artist.

About to unleash scorn on him, she looked into his eyes and saw that he was playing with her. He was smitten with her and prepared to show it. That was all it took: the sincerity not to hide how incredibly enchanting he found her from that first moment. He saw the sincerity in her eyes, too, as she looked above his dark-brown beard and saw eyes as sensitive as hers. It was then he asked how much the modeling payment would be: "*Cuanto dinero?*" She wrinkled her mouth and nose in disgust that he had pushed the joke a step too far and yet felt flattered that he would prefer to attempt to make her smile with his humor, weak as it was.

He lurched toward inviting her to dinner. "*Come conmigo?*" he said, shoveling with a pretend fork toward his mouth and looking at her hopefully.

"*Si, si,*" she had said, sensing it was the best, and perhaps the only, way to free herself of him. She could agree to a plan and then, as seemed reasonable at the moment, break it. His eyes lit up, and he tried one last Spanish question about where dinner should be: "*Donde nos podemos ver?*"

She gave him a knowing look before answering in nearly unaccented English: "Do you know La Paz? I will be there at seven o'clock, and when you meet me for a drink, we can decide where to eat." His eyes opened wide, listening to her speak his language three or four times better than he spoke hers.

"I know La Paz," he said. "I will see you at seven!" Then he had bounced away, surfboard in hand.

In the end, surprising herself, she went.

It was a whirlwind romance. Michael had come to Chile only partly for the waves; the weightier reason was a volcano that had a unique interplay between its glacier and its eruptions. Similar pairings of fire and ice had sparked his imagination before he turned ten, and he became one of the world's experts in anticipating eruptions based on collaborative work performed with glaciologists. Juanita could listen to him talk about it for as long as he wanted as they lay in each other's arms and watched the curtains billow into her bedroom. For he might have been talking about the creative life; he was talking about the creative life, even if he didn't know it.

Each had seen too many instances of love plus time equals destruction among family, friends, and neighbors to contemplate being in the affair full-time. It was one of the only perfect things in either of their lives, and they had returned to it intermittently for all these years. She met him at a conference in Iceland once. The weather was depressing, but she found the geothermal activity other-worldly and beautiful, and their lovemaking entered a new dimension. She also came down with the worst cold of her life and had chosen to leave a day early for fear of getting sicker still in this strange land that married heaven and hell.

The last thing she expected when going out with Maria that night was seeing the love of her life die on television. There was a context for it, but nowhere near enough. During their third interlude (in Seattle), Michael told her about the corruption of his branch of science, and science generally, for the first time. He told her of the depth of pain it caused him. He had all but shown her the door after explaining his thoughts to her, assuming her reaction would be negative. He knew she was apolitical, but he also knew that most artists and educated people were global warming believers.

She didn't like what he told her that day: a congregation of forces (as opposed to a conspiracy) had led to a situation in which the funding of scientists, the reelection of a large group of politicians, and the survival of a few media dinosaurs, including the *New York Times* and the *Washington Post* in his country, had become dependent on a narrative of climate doom. A conspiracy *had* begun to form, though, when former communists from Eastern Bloc countries started calling themselves "greens" and demanded increasingly draconian modifications to capitalism in the name of "saving the planet." He told her they were green on the outside and red on the inside (communist) and that some called them "watermelons." He looked at her with a mix of seriousness and fear when he had said the word "watermelon," sure she would find it offensive, no matter what she said about any lack of politics. She looked back at him with an inscrutable poker face and let him writhe for a few minutes.

"I share values with the people you are talking about, even though I don't care very much about politics," she told him. "But I have seen distortions in my own country; I have seen the way what you call watermelons lie to the native people and use them for their political purposes. That makes my stomach turn."

Their love had survived.

She still lived in the apartment where she and Miguel had ended their first date; he had always loved it. She knew he had barely survived threats to his livelihood at the University of Wyoming over his views, with friends of his having placed the knife in his back on more than one occasion. It had left his heart covered with scar tissue in his dealings with nearly everyone other than herself, but that had meant the tenderness they shared was meaningful to them both. Though without a television at the apartment, she had a Wi-Fi router, which she allowed herself to boot up about once a month, which she did on this strangest of nights. When she got her computer connected to the Internet, she found numerous sites dishing up the video of her lover's death. He looked strong and handsome at the beginning, and he looked like a vulnerable child felled by some strange accident when it ended. She was no crier, not usually. He had only seen her shed tears two or three times in a twenty-five-year relationship. But she wept now.

When it had passed, she moved from the kitchen table, where her laptop was, to her easel, situated to maximize the natural light coming through two of the large windows of her loft apartment. It was 8:30 on a summer evening; the sun would set in a half hour. The light on the mountains was as beautiful as anything on Earth. The oranges and reds had inspired many of her best works at their genesis. She placed a photograph of Miguel next to her canvas and began sketching, half from memory and half from the photograph. Just after the last light shone on the mountains, she leaned back to look at the drawing, uttered a "hmmm" of assent, and put down her pencil. It would do. She squeezed paint from metal tubes onto her palette. By midnight, she had already put on a tolerable first layer. Not only did it look like him, but it had his living presence—the mark of worthwhile art.

After five hours of dream-filled sleep, she was back painting, a mug of coffee beside her. She transferred the brush from her right hand to her left and took sips while checking the painting's progress in the developing morning light. After a piece of toast at 8:30, which she ate standing at her kitchen counter, she sat down to apply the finishing touches. Her signature was the use of hyper-realism in combination with visible, careful brush strokes that Van Gogh would have appreciated. Upon awakening, she realized that she would, for the first time in her career, add a single piece of writing in all capitals to the portrait before digitizing it and sending it into the world. Her tolerance for social media was thin, but some influential artists followed her; everything was aligned to support the statement she had chosen to make when she saw Miguel's body on TV.

5

Ben and Erica were eating locally famous Cuban rice and beans, brought to them by a production assistant, when Erica rested her fork amid beans, yellow rice, plantains, and hot sauce, preparing to speak. They were eating in her office, door open (affair rumors were annoying), and window shades open (both loved the view).

"It's a freaking hoax," she said.

"Yeah?" Ben said.

"Yeah, there's no body."

"I know what I saw," Ben said.

"You think you know what you saw," she said.

"You think O'Brien's alive?" Ben said.

"Maybe," Erica said. "I'm saying there's no body."

"I'm not sure you know that."

Erica picked up her fork, took a bite, and talked while chewing, covering her mouth with the hand holding the fork.

"Well, I know I'm on this as soon as we're done here."

Ben tapped at his computer keyboard, with his lunch set out of the way.

"Well, there appears to be a funeral...tomorrow...in San Diego...where he seems to be from," he said.

"And that's proof of death?"

"It's close," he said.

"Who the hell kills himself because he thinks global warming is B.S.?" she said.

"Um, this guy?" Ben said.

"Maybe," Erica said. "I'm going to the funeral."

"You really loved him, huh?"

"What a total freak show this all is," she said. "Do you know how many texts I've gotten from family asking if this guy was right about what he said?"

"Three?"

"More like thirty," Erica said, taking her last bite.

A nervous hand knocked on the inside of the door frame; it was Erica's assistant, Nan, in a black sweater with black pants and black Chuck Taylors, all in service of her red lipstick that popped beneath her intelligent blue eyes. She had something to say, but she would wait until asked to speak, among her better qualities as an assistant.

"Yes, dear?" Erica said.

"Um, there's another one," Nan said, "in Tibet."

"Tibet?" Erica said.

"Yep," Nan said.

"And we've got it?" Erica said.

"We have it; it's showing in most of Asia," Nan said.

"Who's the guy?" Ben said.

"Another scientist," Nan said, "a moderately big-deal Tibetan climatologist." She held up a thumb drive.

"And have you watched it?" Erica said, holding out her hand. Nan crossed the room in a rush, dropping the drive in her boss's hand and then retreating to the door frame.

"Yes," Nan said from the door.

"And?" Erica said.

"And I don't think this will be the last one," Nan said.

"Jesus," Ben said.

"Thank you, Nan," Erica said as Nan disappeared.

Erica wheeled her chair to Ben's side of the desk as he placed the drive next to his laptop, which paired with it after he pushed a few keys.

"Here we go," he said.

"I hate these guys," Erica said.

"YouTube should ban them," Ben said.

"I'm sure it already has," Erica said.

As the video came to life, parts of it were familiar. There was a lab, a serious-looking man on a folding chair, and the same set of readings on the time-temperature stamp. The only change was that the room's ambient temperature was showing as 15 degrees Celsius, and the thermometer on the scientist showed 37 degrees Celsius. You could see he was about to start speaking from how he looked into the camera.

"Turn on the sound," Erica said.

"It's on," Ben said, "but I'll turn it up." For some reason, the man on the video spoke in what must have been Tibetan. He probably spoke at least some English, like most scientists, but there were English subtitles that he had programmed the equipment to create or that someone else had added.

"My name is Dema Choedrak," the subtitles said. "In my home culture, the only name I need is Dema."

Three fans were on lab tables, pointed toward him, not far from where he sat. He appeared to be in his early sixties; he had close-cropped, white hair, a gray goatee, and beautiful, sad brown eyes behind John Lennon glasses. He wore shorts, a well-worn faded-blue T-shirt, and flip-flops.

"For fifteen years," the subtitles' translation of the man went on, "every step forward my people have taken toward modernity, prosperity, and warm homes has been opposed by people in the West. Such Westerners cajole China to 'keep Tibet pure.' That means China pocketed a billion dollars every year in the name of 'green development'; meanwhile, my people shivered in poorly heated dwellings so that other people could enjoy our 'purity.' My grandparents died in cold homes insufficiently heated by dung fires; their grandparents died in cold homes.

"I will not stand by and watch as even more Tibetans die in cold homes because a comfortable Westerner thinks he's in an oven on a planet whose average temperature would freeze him to death, as it is about to do to me. If this Westerner is young, he perhaps cannot be blamed for his delusion. But if he is my age or older, he likely knew this was a path of deception long ago. And he should have known that this deception had consequences.

"My study of Tibet's past and present climate confirms that the current conditions in our country are not outside the bounds of historical occurrence. My people are strong after surviving so many thousands of years in the Himalayas. But we will not be kept in Third World conditions to make people in the West feel better about themselves. Those in my family know how I feel about them, and to the extent they understand how dire this situation truly is for us and others threatened by the lies of the Climatists, I know they support what I am doing. I have had a wonderful, almost perfect, life."

Unlike O'Brien's check-ins, which came every three hours, Choedrak's came every four. Despite his absence of body fat, he figured that having spent most of his life in a place where an indoor temperature of 59 degrees was a rare luxury, he would retain heat better than someone who had spent their life living in comfort. If, as he expected, it took him longer to die, he didn't want people to endure too many check-ins.

"He seems kind of awesome," Ben said before the first check-in started.

"As psychopaths go, he's charming," Erica said, "which is why what he's doing is so evil."

At the four-hour check-in point, Choedrak was on the familiar folding chair. He had been playing with a Rubik's cube, which he held as he addressed the camera. His temperature was 36.1 degrees Celsius.

"Pause it," Erica said. "What is that in Fahrenheit?"

Ben paused the video; using another browser, he looked up Celsius-to-Fahrenheit conversions.

"Ninety-seven," he said, leaving the page in the background and pressing PLAY.

"I may or may not shiver," Choedrak said, "which, although involuntary, carries shame in my culture."

"This one is worse," Ben said.

"Way," Erica said.

Nan reappeared in the doorway. Ben pushed PAUSE.

Erica looked Nan's way, encouraging her to speak with her eyebrows raised inquisitively.

"They have a name for them now," Nan said.

"But there are only two of them," Ben said.

"They're calling them the Fifty-Niners, because—"

"Because that's the temperature they use to kill themselves, like their own effed-up Hamburger Hill," Ben said.

Erica looked at him quizzically.

"Vietnam," Ben said.

"I'm aware of the battle," Erica said. "Weird reference?"

"Sure," Ben said.

He pushed PLAY.

The video was at the eight-hour point, the Tibetan's second

check-in. At first glance, it appeared Choedrak still was looking directly into the camera. But as he began to speak, it became clear that he was reading from a teleprompter or cue card he had set up for himself.

"I am uncomfortable in my body but at peace in my heart. I am uncomfortable in my body but at peace in my heart. I am uncomfortable in my body but at peace in my heart." Even though he was repeating the words robotically, he felt what the words meant; you could see that in his eyes.

"Jesus," Ben said.

"Shit," Erica said.

His body temperature sensor said 33.9.

"Temperature?" Erica said.

"Ninety-three," Ben said.

"Shouldn't he be in, like, a coma by now?" Erica said.

"I don't know a lot about it," Ben said.

Choedrak's belief that he would retain his body heat longer than someone from a warm climate was only partly borne out. If it had mattered, it had helped by a half-degree. Meanwhile, his culturally acquired lack of a shiver response had done much harm. With the "wind" hitting him and his lack of body fat, his core temperature was plummeting. His would not be a longer video than O'Brien's, not at the current rate.

The twelve-hour check-in revealed a familiar scene: a scientist on the floor next to a chair. The only surprise was that he had taken off his clothes, as a percentage of people with hypothermia do. Someone had blurred Choedrak's middle section strategically before the video was distributed, which was significant because it could mean he had co-conspirators. It could also just mean that the Asian television networks got the tape first and had added the layer of digital modesty.

The body thermometer showed 30.6 degrees Celsius; Ben noted Erica was glancing at it, and he brought the conversions browser forward without being asked.

"Eighty-seven degrees," he said, pressing PLAY.

"Wait," Erica said. "And he's naked because?"

"People with hypothermia do that sometimes," Ben said.

"Sheesh," Erica said. Ben again pressed PLAY.

The scene was as before but seeing Choedrak on the floor nude a second time humanized him in a way that was hard to brush aside. They were looking at a person who had given his life to save science and his fellow Tibetans, or at least in his own mind. The thermometer showed 28 degrees Celsius; the pulsometer, 0.

"Still going to O'Brien's funeral?" Ben asked.

"I guess not," Erica said.

It had been a difficult day, and it wasn't yet one o'clock. Nan reappeared, her body in the doorway an implied question.

"Sutcliffe wants to see us?" Erica said. Nan nodded in confirmation and left.

The fact that neither was talking as they walked down the hallway surprised them. It was as though there had been a death in the family for one, or both, of them.

Sutcliffe had two other producers seated in his office—Rita Guzman and Steve Tripp—who had been with the show for a decade. Guzman worked her way up from the inside after starting like Nan. Steve had come from CBS, where he had won two Emmys before he was thirty-five with *Sixty Minutes*. He was compact and athletic-looking, with salt-and-pepper hair and expensive-looking black-framed glasses.

Sutcliffe indicated that Ben and Erica should sit. They could see through the picture window behind him the limestone façade of the Associated Press building, in the same Art-Deco style as the building where the three of them worked.

"How does this change things?" Sutcliffe asked.

"There's still no proof of death for either one," Erica said.

"You think they were faked?" Sutcliffe said.

"There's no way those suicides were faked, dear," Guzman said. Of all the producers in the room, and in the building for that matter, she was the cagiest. Her rise from within had forced her to take on a type of shrewdness that most people could not. She would have risen fast if she wasn't green-eyed, red-haired, and sexy, but it would have been more challenging.

"And your proof is?" Erica said.

"My proof is we're in Chip's office, and the five of us have never met here, and you know in your heart that this isn't bullshit."

"Maybe I do," Erica said. "But won't we all be feeling funny if it turns out that these dudes are having a drink in a tropical bar someplace, laughing their asses off?"

"Ladies, what you both say makes sense to me," Sutcliffe said. "And I would like proof of death as soon as possible. As we're working on proof of death, I need the four of you to work on separate stories about their backgrounds and how and where they may have interacted before if they did. We have two tapes like this in three days."

"O'Brien's funeral is tomorrow in San Diego," Erica said.

"We'll have multiple crews on hand for that," Sutcliffe said. "In the meantime, on teases and the broadcast until further notice, just leave an escape hatch: 'Scientist X, who *apparently* took his own life.'"

"Roger that," Ben said.

6

While he lived, Michael O'Brien knew that there were people around the globe, probably a good number of them, who would have become volcanologists in the way he had if they had the aptitude. He also knew that if the dreamers were to spend a month camped near the rim of a sulfuric hellscape like Katla, where he had passed the better part of six months in 2025, almost all of them would have reconsidered. Some of his peers said they got used to the stench, but he never adapted to the stomach-churning fumes. The masks kept you safe from the toxicity of the sulfuric gas cocktail on the days when it was dangerous enough to need them, but for him, they *magnified* the smell. He imagined the experience similar to what seafaring pioneers in centuries past went through when suffering of some sort was a given most of the time. On days when the venting of sulfur was minimal or when the wind kept the fumes away, he strangely missed it, for he had come to associate it with productive research. And although they smelled like popular descriptions of hell, the fumes, when present, gave him the sense that it was game-on.

Katla had been a breakthrough success story both in his career and the science of volcanology. In the mid-2020s, seismic sensors indicated large amounts of lava were moving beneath Katla. Teams had been visiting sites around its mouth, with the

Icelandic group keeping researchers in the field without interruption. But with the sensors spiking on December 27, 2024, half a dozen teams arrived from points around the world in the next three weeks.

O'Brien's six-man group—with two each from the University of Glasgow, the University of Washington, and the University of Wyoming—arrived during a snowstorm in mid-January. The scent of air thick with snow and sulfur dioxide was grotesque, though the sulfur levels were not high enough to require masks. The team pitched tents on a promontory surveying a glacial outwash plain. When it was clear, they could see the Atlantic to the south, the volcano to the north, and the glacier's edge a kilometer from their location. The proximity meant transits to and from measuring stations were less taxing than they would have been if they had stayed at any of the nearby villages. It also meant that if the eruption assumed to be approaching progressed too fast, they were at risk of being killed by, among other things, glacial runoff. For them, it was a risk worth running.

Geologists take the long view on climate. As the *New York Times* got more breathless about the last half-century's weather, O'Brien and his friends raised their eyebrows knowingly to one another and let the madness play on. Even though geologists enjoyed some protection from the Climatists' efforts to purge dissent, more than one of them had nonetheless seen the quality of his or her life diminished through public shaming. Being a geologist meant trying to survive climate change, only the changes in climate were moral and intellectual.

Out here on Katla, the intellectual climate was delightful, partly because fellow researchers with whom one could constructively disagree were present. O'Brien would have said this about Seth Pedersen of the University of Glasgow, who had published papers putatively linking climate change to eruption patterns. For a Climatist, he was not strident, and his foundational science was first-rate. Somewhat incredibly, he could even laugh at himself when other team members gave him grief about the climate change bogeyman coming for him in the night. All six of them could laugh at themselves. It was a less rare characteristic among geologists than among, for instance, atmospheric scientists, perhaps in part because they were, on the whole, spinning fewer half-deceptions than their stern-faced brothers and sisters posing with celebrities on the covers of magazines.

There were many reasons for the American team, and all the others, to be at Katla. Historically the most destructive volcano on the island, it had killed tens of thousands of Icelanders over the centuries. Over the millennia, the eruptions of Katla and other Icelandic volcanoes had also proved lethal for large numbers of Europeans on the continent, with sun-shrouding discharges giving rise to withering cold and failed crops. If Katla again delivered in 2025 what it was capable of, every hour of warning the research teams could give the people of Iceland and their European neighbors would save lives. Both their roles as de facto public servants and as pure researchers were meaningful to everyone at the work sites.

O'Brien's and the rest of his team's sensors numbered many dozens; hundreds of sensors, combining those of every team, had been set up in and near the volcano's wide caldera. Thick ice covered the caldera, and the interplay of the ice with underlying heat was O'Brien's expertise. He was working on expanding an idea he had developed while in Chile. The concept was that by observing harmonic tremors below three or more points on a glacier and looking for overlying weakness in the ice in the caldera, one could get an idea about the timing of the eventual eruption. That, in turn, meant gaining time for notifying the public of imminent peril.

The first three months saw a repeating pattern of two harmonic tremors manifesting at inconsistent locations and then receding. For O'Brien, Katla's doings gave him the sense of waiting for an overdue birth or death. At night in the tents, to deal with the sense of a vigil, he and the others talked about sensor failures and battery life and the minutiae of the daily work over plastic bowls of pasta and rehydrated stew.

At 3:17 A.M. on May 18th, during the best weather of the trip, a triple tremor set off notification alarms O'Brien had created for the occasion, waking him from a deep sleep. He pulled on his outerwear and boots, then drove one of the all-terrain vehicles across the uneven land to the nearest sensor in the faint twilight of the sunrise that had already begun. Harmonic tremors on volcanoes, absent ice like at Katla, were relatively undramatic. Still, for reasons yet to be determined—but among them being friction, heat, gravity, and torque—superficial harmonic tremors in the presence of a glacier tended to be more spasmodic. The early-hour event endured for twenty minutes after O'Brien arrived at his sensor, but none of his mapping software found a match between the sub-surface activity and weakness in the ice. When it ended, he climbed into the ATV's seat and looked skyward in frustration. Then he drove back to camp across the gravel and lichen-covered rock, hardly noticing the beautiful sunrise overhead as he concentrated on not rolling the bouncing four-wheeler.

A second triple tremor came just after breakfast eight days later; it felt to O'Brien like it could be the start of something significant. He spent ten hours at the liveliest sensor before the activity ended. A speck on the fringe of an immense sea of ice, O'Brien felt paradoxically disappointed not to have been present for an eruption that would have risked his life. But he had given up his attachment to most of his ego's everyday concerns, including remaining alive. If you paid close attention to them, volcanoes humbled you in a deep place.

Despite the failure of his prediction system to yield positive results and despite the accompanying failure of Katla to erupt, O'Brien remained optimistic. On June 3rd, a new triple harmonic tremor sequence began to unfold. All but one of his seventeen sensors showed shallow tremors simultaneously, and the deeper sensors of his tent-mate, Pedersen, showed a monthslong event peaking. O'Brien radioed the team. This was beyond mapping tremors and ice; this was clearly what had brought them to Iceland.

"It's time to evacuate, folks—over," he said.

He was the only one on the expedition who had been at another glacial-volcano eruption in Kamchatka in 2013, and everyone on Katla took his assessment as a red alert. Still, the walkie-talkies began to crackle with questions from his team members and members of the other teams. (They had agreed to send out an emergency-only Morse code signaling everyone to set walkie-talkies to channel one; accomplishing this had been O'Brien's first step.)

"Come in, Mike," the voice of his best friend on the team, Glenn Stewart, sputtered from O'Brien's walkie-talkie. "Is there time, in your estimation, to retrieve sensors? Over."

"Negative, Glenn, my estimation of event timing is not precise," O'Brien responded, "but that is a negative on retrieval. Over."

"Do you have a number of hours you estimate? Over."

"I'm estimating twelve hours," O'Brien said, "but I'm not pre-pared to give anyone a false sense of security. Over."

"Roger and out," came Stewart's voice.

Someone speaking English with a faint, but indeterminate accent came through O'Brien's walkie-talkie next; it could have been any of two dozen researchers on-site.

"America, what is the basis, please, for evacuation? Over."

"This is Michael O'Brien; who is this, please? Over."

"Apologies, America, this is Hendrik Karlsen with Norway. Over."

"Roger that, Hendrik, no worries, and this is for everyone's benefit, as agreed. Our sensors are on fire down here. We recom-mend full evacuation at top speed. Over."

Ultimately, lava, ash, and mud buried more than five million dollars' worth of equipment. But every visiting scientist had made it off the volcano alive and subsequently off Iceland. They had each kept pricey, open-ended departure tickets on Iceland-air, allowing them to take any available seat on any flight. The Americans, first to the airport, took flights to Oslo; the Norwe-gians went to Dublin; the Danes flew to Manchester; the Finns flew to Toronto; and so on. Only the Icelanders remained, and they probably would have flown somewhere themselves if they had thought to buy plane tickets. It was they, logically, who no-tified local authorities.

The eruption began at 4:13 p.m. with an initial 70,000-vertical-foot thrust of ash, rock, dust, and sulfuric gases. One-third of Iceland's cattle died before sunrise the next day, with the rest suffering pitifully. The great bulk of the public heeded urgent warnings via all media and air-raid sirens repurposed for the emergency to retreat into their homes where they stuffed air gaps with fabric. A couple of hundred homeless people, about ninety percent of the total homeless population in Reykjavik, died painfully in alleys, on park benches, and under highway overpasses. The other ten percent allowed volunteers and police to talk them into going indoors as the poisonous gas was drawing near.

The eruption didn't make the climate debate any more rational, partly because Katla influenced regional weather for two years. Crop yields fell more than fifty percent throughout Europe; bitter Arctic outbreaks made capitals from Paris to Prague seem a part of Siberia; sea ice rendered Iceland's harbors impenetrable for the first time in generations. There were paintings in the great galleries of Europe showing similar conditions hundreds of years earlier. Still, few understood what the images in the paintings suggested about the repetition of weather (and climate) events.

Neither O'Brien nor any of the other volcanologists on Katla wanted hero's medals for a warning that, in the end, had not been able to prevent widespread death and destruction. But in the small volcanology community, O'Brien's rock-star status was solidified.

Nightmarishly, however, it had only taken a couple of weeks for the Climatists to trot out the eruption as presumptive proof of their crisis narrative. The theory they got into the news media was simple: Glaciers the world over had been rendered unstable by rising atmospheric temperatures, and sometimes these glaciers' meltwater flooded volcanoes, causing eruptions like Katla's. The theory was simplistic, manipulative, and wrong. Still, it became a widely held belief among journalists, politicians, the public, and even scientists, never mind that modern-day temperatures were within recent historical bounds and that Katla had been erupting every hundred years throughout known history. O'Brien had no particular thirst to be in the limelight. But for him, the distortions surrounding Katla becoming accepted as fact by virtually everyone he knew turned a scientific victory into a profound disappointment. There was no beating the Climatists in the court of public opinion.

7

Juanita had been to San Diego once before. She and Miguel had stayed at a cute 1950s-era hotel about a block from Pacific Beach. When they tumbled to the bed the first night, she noticed that there were not one, but two longboards propped against the wall. When they were holding each other afterward, with the curtains billowing in as they did in her apartment, she thought to tease him about the second board.

"Are you riding two boards, Miguel?" she asked.

"The last time you came with me somewhere with easy waves you said you would surf one more time," he said. "I brought you one."

"I like owing this to you," she said. "I like your not knowing if it adds to your power over me or lessens it."

"These are serious ideas," he said. "Wouldn't it be easier just to go surfing than to carry such heavy thoughts around?"

"Perhaps, little angel," Juanita said. "We shall see in the morning."

She had gifted him with a surf at dawn the next day, in nicely peeling two-to-three-foot waves, just north of the pier. Miguel told her that her surfing was better than made sense for someone who hadn't been on a board in so long. Though they saw a few other surfers daring some four-footers beside the pilings, neither of the two lovebirds had anything to prove—just the opposite.

They were a happy couple grabbing a few easy rides with the sun rising beyond the hills over their shoulders. The vast Pacific, with pelicans and shorebirds gliding over it, extended in front of them as they waited for sets.

Twenty years later, she was pleased when the clerk told her from San Diego over the phone that they had room 204—her and Miguel's old room—available. Opening the door, she realized there was more space than she needed. But that meant the room was large enough to contain the memories of shared experiences, including those of her last surf. She had never stopped loving riding waves. Instead, a car accident had left her brain about ninety percent of its former self; there was nothing science could do for the last ten percent, and the doctors impressed on her the importance of avoiding reinjury. She loved the sport, but she loved being clear minded more. It was a painful loss. After checking in alone and going up to the room, she was still unsure if she would surf alone here to honor their history. She might, and then again, she might not. There was Miguel's funeral to get through in the meantime.

Already the post of her painting of him was blowing up on various platforms. People could say what they wanted about Miguel's motivations or his supposed lack of climate expertise; she had painted a man with a fine mind and a beautiful heart, and no one could take her memories of him away from her. She had nearly painted the word *martyr* on the canvas before photographing it; in the end, she had chosen something more humanizing: MICHAEL.

Although she surmised that the Climatists would have people at the funeral, her thoughts about what that might mean were vague. The service would be at 10:00 A.M. At 9:00, she was tucking the painting, wrapped in canvas secured with twine, into the trunk of an Uber that took her the three miles north to St. James by-the-Sea Church in La Jolla.

As a woman who barely followed politics, she was only distantly aware of the forces that had turned her beloved's journey on the planet into one marked by strife and hardship. She did not know, for instance, that groups backed by left-wing billionaires had put out ad-hominem hit jobs on climate dissenters the moment they outed themselves. She did not know that books by Climatists and politicians on the topic of global warming were generally ghost-written by staff members at the groups rather than by the scientists and politicians themselves. She vaguely apprehended "spontaneous" demonstrations protesting the continued use of fossil fuels and other intelligent forms of modernity had been orchestrated by a non-governmental politburo of leftists at the time and location deemed most advantageous to the cause. She didn't know that bullying and intimidation the Climatists considered justified had ruined thousands of careers, destroyed families, and ended lives. That was because she hadn't taken the time to understand the combination of bourgeois guilt and elitist snobbery underlying the political apparatus the Climatists had constructed.

But now she could hear the apparatus through the open window of her Uber as it made its way to within two blocks of the church. Traffic had thickened in the last quarter mile, and there were police barricades ahead. The driver, a middle-aged surfer by the look of him, had taken note of the circumstances.

"It might save you time to walk," he said. "Do you want me to get you closer?"

"I'll walk," she said. "Could you get me to the curb so I can retrieve my painting?"

"Of course."

It was awkward walking into a crowd with a painting two-thirds her height in her hands. She nestled it under one arm like a surfboard, steadying it with her other hand. As she passed a handful of satellite trucks parked end to end, she saw a dozen more jammed into side streets and felt her stomach knot up. People she took to be Miguel's relatives milled in the foyer; she could see his coffin in the front of the church, a cream-colored pall over it. Although it was 9:30, the closest spot to sit was ten or twelve rows from the front. She had thought through what to do with the painting, understanding that such a large object would be distracting and awkward during the ceremony. The idea she came up with was simple. Church offices were usually left unlocked during services, at least in Chile. Would an Episcopal church in America be the same? It was. She turned the doorknob, opened the door hesitantly as though expecting to find someone inside, and met a startled female priest, Canon Becky Picerne.

"I am so sorry," Juanita said. "This is a painting of Michael that I have made. Could I leave it here during the service?"

A middle-aged grandmother with bottle-blond hair and sky-blue eyes, Picerne had the gravitas of a true believer about to facilitate the passage of a human soul to heaven.

"That would be fine," she said, pulling just enough warmth into her eyes not to appear harsh. Her cream-colored vestment matched the pall over the casket.

"I cannot thank you enough," Juanita said. "I am so sorry to disturb you."

"You did not disturb me one bit," Picerne said. "The door will be open after the service for half an hour."

"You are saving me," Juanita said.

"Well, that's my job," Picerne said, and now her priestly

warmth was in full force. Sitting in a pew, Juanita replayed the interchange in her mind, vaguely worrying whether she had frightened the priest. Three rows at the front of the church bore ribbons to reserve them for family. Five minutes before ten o'clock, two people Juanita took to be Miguel's parents settled in the front pew. Although grief-stricken, they were tan and healthy-looking and clearly a comfort to each other. Then she realized this could not be his two parents, who had divorced when he was a young teenager. The gray-haired man looked too much like Miguel not to be his father, which meant that the attractive woman sitting beside him must be the stepmother. The gray-haired couple across the aisle from Miguel's father partially blocked Juanita's line of sight. Still, she knew these two were likely the mother and stepfather. She couldn't remember if the stepparents were the same ones the parents had left each other for; the whole thing had been a mess. She was amazed that a church was willing to hold the funeral. Though a lapsed Catholic, Juanita had vestiges of church dogma in her deepest fibers, having grown up devout in a family that included priests. The idea that church elders would grant a suicide a funeral such as this back home was unthinkable, modernity's encroaching power notwithstanding. Organ music interrupted the train of her thoughts, and she saw that the church had filled in, even to the point of overflowing. Did Miguel know so many people? Had people who supported his actions come to pay their respects?

Whoever might be present, the congregation had taken its feet and was breaking into the first bars of "Amazing Grace"; harmonizing comfortably, the priest trailed the choir as it processed up the center aisle. No singer, Juanita nonetheless reached for a hymnal and joined in. None of this was going the way she imagined.

8

"Good morning!" said the rector, now entirely in her element. A dozen white-robed acolytes stood nearby on the dais as she spoke from behind O'Brien's casket.

"Good morning!" responded most of the hundreds of people present. Still startled by the scale and friendly atmosphere of the event, Juanita wasn't among those who returned the greeting.

"I am Canon Becky Picerne, the rector at St. James by-the-Sea." She was wearing a nearly invisible microphone, and her confident voice was carried well in the church so that even the people standing in the back could hear her. "It wasn't long ago, and even at the beginning of my career as a priest, that we had to dance around the subjects of mental health and suicide when we wanted to give a church service to someone who had taken their own life. When my father was a young priest in the Episcopal Church, the only possible way to have a funeral for someone who had committed suicide was to pretend that we did not know how the person died or that they had died from something other than the true cause. We were doing our best, but it's clear now we added to the sorrow of families who had lost a loved one in such a painful way.

"But today we are here to celebrate the good life of Michael O'Brien. I have been proud to count myself a friend of Michael's and of his family for most of my career at St. James. He was a remarkable young man who was no less remarkable the day he died. We would have been out of luck if we had to pretend that he hadn't taken his own life, as, strangely enough, many of you here have seen the videotape of his last hours. That's modernity for you." (This elicited a few knowing smiles and a nervous titter of laughter.)

"Please refer to your leaflets, page one, for our opening prayer."

For the next twenty minutes, Juanita's awareness drifted from the sun-drenched panels of stained glass to the prayers the assembled recited, to the hymns they sang, to those around her in the pews, to Miguel's coffin, to her encounter with the canon, to what she would do when the service ended. After the priest had read the gospel, she launched into her sermon; here, Juanita was paying attention. The priest began with an allusion to the service's Old Testament reading.

"'The steadfast love of the Lord never ceases; his mercies never come to an end.' These are beautiful words, and for those of us in the Christian faith community, they are more than that. They are a living reality, although one that is hard to remember. For in the course of our lives, more than ever during this electronic time in which we live, we have all been buffeted by strong winds that would blow us away from the remembrance of God's love for us. And so it is with every person who takes their own life, whatever reasons they may have believed they had at the time. Michael was a gifted person devoted to furthering scientific knowledge and helping his fellow man. But even one as brilliant as Michael can fall victim to the winds we all know are blowing across computer screens and smartphones, with lies and distortions so overwhelming that they can undo even the best of us.

"The gospel of John we read today points us in a like direction. Jesus said, 'Very truly, I tell you, anyone who hears my word and believes him who sent me has eternal life, and does not come under judgment, but has passed from death to life.' We are not here, I am not here, to pass judgment on a man as good as Michael. Something happened, something most of us will fortunately never understand, that caused him to forget that God's 'mercies never come to an end.' Do we wish he had never had thoughts put in his head by someone probably less noble and intelligent than himself to make him doubt the science of which he was a living emblem? Of course, we do! But that is something different, brothers and sisters, from passing judgment on one of our own, from daring to pass judgment on a man who lived in the service of what we Episcopalians refer to as 'this fragile earth, our island home.' Michael's undoing was proof of that fragility, which we all carry within us, and which God wishes us to be aware of, in the form of compassion, for ourselves and others."

One row behind Juanita's and on the other side of the center aisle, two men and three women, all seemingly black-clad mourners, stood. They raised large hand-lettered signs over their heads reading "CRIMINAL!" and began chanting: "Deniers are liars…deniers go to Hell! Deniers are liars…deniers go to Hell!"

For a moment, the entire congregation was stunned. Overwhelmed by the rudeness and sounds coming out of the protestors' mouths, Juanita wasn't surprised by what they were expressing. Miguel had explained the lengths to which the Climatists had taken their fight against those who dared oppose them. He would have been flattered they had made it their business to ruin his funeral; it meant he had gotten to them. The protesters were on their sixth time through their incantation before church elders, now de facto security, pulled them out of the pew and marched them up the center aisle. Sheriff's deputies who'd hesitated to use force during a church service promptly cuffed them and led them out through the main doors. Loud murmuring rose from the assembled, and Juanita saw anxiety and faith compete for dominance on the priest's face.

"Michael's decisions at the end of his life have occasioned strong feelings," Canon Picerne said. "Let us see if we can regain the spirit of love with which we choose to honor him in this place. Heavenly Father, help us remember what is good about one another; help us remember who we are in your eyes; help us remember that in the fullness of time, all sorrows are in line to be healed by your tenderest mercies through Christ our Lord. Amen." Most in the pews joined in the "amen," and the ugliness of the interruption seemed to have been healed.

"I know that friends and family of Michael's wish to say a few words," the canon said. "First, we have Michael's younger brother, David." With this, a tall, bearded man sitting near Michael's mother stood. He had lighter coloring than Michael, who could have passed as Chilean with native blood, as Juanita had told him, but there was a resemblance in the hairline, the shape of the jaw, the broad shoulders, and the presence. It was plain that the two of them were close from how the brother walked to the pulpit.

He stood behind the podium and allowed himself to take in the multitude of those assembled while he drew a few breaths. He returned the sorrowful, warm looks coming to him from around the church.

"My brother was not crazy," he said, "not on the day he died or any other day. Thank you for coming." He returned to his spot in the front row and sat down.

Several people spoke of Michael, all movingly. Juanita learned things about him he had never told her. He rescued a robin with a broken wing when he was seven years old. When a buddy lost the use of his legs after a skateboarding accident, Michael never rode his own again—not for fear of the danger but in solidarity with a friend who would never have the pleasure. He was the rare nerd on whom a surprising number of girls had crushes in high school. All the things Juanita learned made sense, and she found that she was, against her better judgment, falling in love with him in a new way.

The only speaker to outdo Michael's brother in brevity was his mother. She walked, head high, to the pulpit, despite the evident effort, and said: "Michael was a good son."

After the Mass concluded and the acolytes had put the wine and wafers away, the organist broke into "The Strife is Over." The choir led the congregation through the last three verses as, in their crimson and white robes, they recessed up the center aisle, followed by a server carrying the processional cross, followed by the other servers, and finally, the priest. It was surprising, Juanita realized, as she did her best to sing a hymn she did not know, that there hadn't been more than one priest officiating. Perhaps, she thought, this was the only sign of shame at this funeral for a suicide.

The family filed out behind the priest. Suddenly, Juanita remembered the television crews and the likelihood of renewed conflict and felt brief panic over the fact that someone might have locked the office door and made it impossible to get back the painting. Politely but firmly, she slipped past those slowly shuffling up the side aisle and told herself that the priest's assurance the door would remain unlocked had been sincere.

It had been. The painting leaned against built-in bookshelves, right where Juanita had left it. Through the closed window, she heard the muffled sound of chanting. Those who were making the sounds, it was clear, were individuals who considered Michael to have been sub-human. She might have had the pluck to fight them on their own terms if they had been Chileans speaking Spanish. But here, in this odd country where suicides were allowed proper funerals and protesters felt free to interrupt a requiem Mass, it was too daunting. The shouting and chanting grew louder as she joined the last people filing out of the church.

She blinked through the first few moments in the bright sun before seeing that the priest and Michael's family had formed a receiving line on the left side of the stairs, with Canon Picerne standing closest to her. Meanwhile, there were a few dozen protesters on the lawn in front of the church; they held overhead neon-hued posterboard signs with black lettering that made their feelings clear:

DEAD BUT NOT FORGIVEN

FIFTY-NINERS ROT IN HELL

DENIERS ARE LIARS! DENIERS GO TO HELL!!

IT'S NOT NICE TO FOOL MOTHER NATURE

With fury on their faces and expensive casual clothing on their backs, they yelled the same thing their recently arrested brothers and sisters had shouted in the church: "Deniers are liars; deniers go to Hell!" The overall effect was to make Juanita feel exhausted. Then it came to her that she possessed her own sign. Stepping as far from the receiving line as possible to avoid disrupting it, the brokenhearted Chilean kept high enough on the stairs to be visible to everyone below. She uncovered her painting and lifted it over her head.

The dynamic in front of the church shifted. Cameras that had been shooting protesters and the receiving line turned toward

her, first a few, then the rest. The protesters, most veteran dem-
onstrators, were canny enough to recognize that anyone in the
media turning away from them was a bad thing. And when they
looked up and saw this beautiful mixed-race South American
woman with a portrait she had evidently painted herself, with
the first name of the man who had done this horrible thing
along its lower third, they began to shout, "No!"

Juanita learned that a couple of dozen voices projecting ill
intent in one's direction was frightening, all the more when the
people yelling appeared to be on the verge of losing control. A
beautiful, self-important female journalist with a microphone in
hand and a cameraman and a producer in tow crossed and
climbed the stairs in her direction. Juanita had anticipated this
but had no idea what she would say in response to any questions. In a matter of moments, the journalist had introduced
herself as Claudia Bowers with CNN and had put a microphone
in front of Juanita's face.

"Did you know O'Brien?" Bowers asked.

"Yes," Juanita said.

"How did you know him?"

"We met on one of his scientific trips to my country."

"What country is that?"

"Chile; he came to look at our glacial volcanoes."

"Was he your boyfriend?"

"You could say so."

"What is your name?"

Juanita had opened her mouth to respond when she saw a
woman with long, gray-blond hair wearing a wine-colored dress
and tan Birkenstocks had crept behind the CNN team. The
woman rushed forward, took the painting from Juanita's hands,
and brought it down on her head, tearing the canvas and leaving

Juanita within the frame. A cheer rose among the protesters, the first happy sound they had made. Although she had done nothing wrong, Juanita knew shame she hadn't felt since childhood. When the CNN reporter began to address her again, Juanita held up one hand to indicate that the interview was over. She pulled the frame back over her head, then told two police officers already cuffing the woman who'd destroyed her painting that she preferred not to press charges. Juanita was so disoriented that, for a moment, it seemed Michael was walking toward her from the other side of the steps. After gathering herself, she realized it was Michael's brother who had spoken first at the funeral.

"I'm David," he said. "Are you okay?"

"Not really," Juanita said.

"I can imagine," he said. "Mike talked about you."

Tears came to her eyes.

"I know he couldn't let you get close," David said, "but I also know you were the love of his life."

"Thank you," Juanita said. "You're very kind."

"Would you like to meet the family?"

"It's too much," Juanita said. "I am sorry. I know you need to go to the cemetery."

"Not at all," David said, "he would have understood, and so do I. You're right about the cemetery; my sister is giving me the stare-down. I know it doesn't feel like it, but your painting is the thing that will have mattered here this morning. It's what people will remember."

"That, too, is kind," Juanita said.

"You may hear from me," he said as he began to join the family.

"That would be fine," Juanita said.

She walked a half mile away before summoning an Uber. The

idea of dropping the destroyed painting near a trash container occurred to her more than once. She didn't trust herself to know if it was a decision she would regret. For the second time in one day, she opened the trunk of a strange car and put her painting inside. Michael's painted right eye, on a piece of canvas folded at a right angle where it had been torn, looked up at her as she closed the trunk hatch. Sitting in the rear passenger seat, she felt a need to paddle out into the waves they had once shared, even if it turned out that she was too upset actually to catch one.

The driver, South American like her, pulled the vehicle to a stop in front of the hotel. She thanked him, went to the hatchback, grabbed what remained of the painting, and went into the lobby. Avoiding the clerk's glance, she pushed the button for the elevator, entered it, and pressed the button for her floor, exhaling for what seemed the first time in a long while as the elevator rose. After letting herself in the room, she stashed the painting, changed clothes, and left the room again within ten minutes. She took the stairs to the lobby and walked to a surf shop two doors away, where they rented boards and wetsuits. She chose a wetsuit and a longboard for $70 for two hours and then returned to the hotel to stash her wallet and pull on the neoprene suit.

When her bare feet hit the pleasantly warm sand, she jogged the hundred yards to the water. Sitting on the sea-foam-green rented board, she was just an anonymous person in a black wetsuit harmonizing with the ocean; in the end, she caught several waves.

By the time she walked through the surf shop's door to return the board, the recent moments of self-forgetfulness were fading. The store felt different than it had two hours before.

"Are you that Fifty-Niner's girlfriend?" the tattooed, blond high-school girl behind the counter who'd rented her the board with a cheerful smile two hours before asking her. "Because that's really fucked up." Somehow, the local surfer girl had become a self-styled Grand Inquisitor. CNN wasn't on the television, which had a surf video playing, but what had gone down that morning was not only international news but local news as well. Three of the surf shop employee's friends had texted her a link to the painting-smash video while Juanita had been out in the waves washing off what felt like a layer of filth.

"Thank you for the rental," Juanita said. She flashed the girl a look that said roughly, "You probably don't want to mess with this," and then walked out the door.

9

"Don't even think about being the next Fifty-Niner," a simmering Amy said to Whit. A moment earlier, he had been alone in the kitchen making them coffee; now, he had what looked like a lioness protecting her cubs, poking her finger in his direction. Not all mornings were born equal.

"You knew him, didn't you?" she said.

Up to then, there had been a total of thirteen Fifty-Niners. It had been four months since O'Brien had become the first. She might have meant any of Whit's friends who had videoed their deaths from hypothermia while exposed to the planet's average temperature for less than a day. But he was willing to guess that his distraught wife meant the most recent one: Luigi Corso, a renowned Italian volcanologist whom Whit had known reasonably well. Whit's hazel eyes registered confusion, which Amy rightly took as a feint.

"You know who I mean," she said.

"Listen, I have nothing to hide, and I love you," Whit said. "I haven't had my coffee, and you haven't had yours. What if we sit down and have a conversation?"

She looked at him with eyes of mistrust but let him put her coffee mug in her hands. They sat on the kitchen's dilapidated antique sofa they were always talking about having reupholstered. It had been with them as graduate students, and now it was in their A-frame house in a neighborhood dense with faculty families. The sofa hadn't impressed any of their friends in its vintage incarnation, but they had drunk a lot of coffee while sitting on its horsehair upholstery, and they were partial to it. He had a quick swallow from the mug of coffee and remembered telling her about the careful process of his and Mike determining that they could trust each other.

"Okay, I remember," he said. "I knew more than one of them; I was confused."

"Yes, you did," she said, the sharper edges of her hostility already sanded down by coffee.

"But you're talking about Mike O'Brien, the first one," he said.

"Yes, I am," she said. "You liked O'Brien; it came to me in the night that you two thought of this. By the way, Jacob kept me up from one to three."

The morning he was having was starting to make sense. Indeed, he and O'Brien had discussed fighting back against the Climatists, walking over a glacier and over a Chinese chess board Whit had brought to Antarctica.

"People think of a lot of things in the middle of the night," Whit said, shifting beside her.

"You're on thin ice, brother," she said.

"This is war, and I'm not talking about between you and me," he said.

"You've said that before; you're going to need to tell me something new before the kids get up," she said. "Jacob was stirring when I came down."

"It wasn't just Mike and me," he said. "And it was agreed from the start that no one with kids would be allowed to do the experiment."

"It's not an experiment," she said. She looked Whit's way with menace.

"That is true," he said. "But getting everything set up the correct way is less straightforward than you might think."

"And?"

"I know you get it," he said. "I know you know the person will always die."

"You said *person* rather than *man*. Tell me no women are in on this."

"There are women," Whit said.

"Jesus, Whit!"

"You act as if women have more to lose than men who give up their lives to try to save science," he said. "You care that much about science yourself, only you're a mom now."

"So, no moms?"

"No moms," he said.

"You're still out of your minds."

"If the death of science before one's own eyes isn't enough to drive you crazy, then you're not paying attention."

"That sounds heroic, but you listen to me," she said. "If you become a Fifty-Niner and leave the kids and me behind, I will come and find you in hell, and I will kill you myself again."

He paused. "I hear you," he said.

"I'm not kidding," she said. "Find another way to matter, something more intelligent than martyrdom."

"We talked about it and thought about it for a long time," he said. "The Climatists have won, basically. Our ambition is to leave a trace of awareness of what science *was* so that someone can re-create it decades from now."

"I'll kill you again," she said. "Don't doubt it for a minute. By the way, I know you think you can change hearts and minds in this generation. You probably secretly hope you'll be able to continue with your pure research. Was that hope worth letting friends of yours die? Is that your nobility?"

As he had learned, marriage is not for the faint of heart.

"So, I'm a bastard if I become a Fifty-Niner, and I'm a bastard if I don't," he said. "Have I got it right?"

"You don't have anything right," she said. "There has always been on this earth what is and what should be, and people who die to make it be what it should be are generally assholes who care only about themselves."

"I'll be sure to tell Jesus," Whit said.

"If you become a Fifty-Niner, I'm pretty sure the two of you won't be having any face-to-face conversations."

"Do you know how many people died from cold in the United Kingdom last year?"

"Too many?"

"Fifty-three thousand."

"And?"

"And absent the Climatists' forcing Britain to abandon fossil fuels before they had a legitimate replacement, about forty thousand of those people would still be alive today. A few on fixed incomes always left their thermostats lower than their bodies could handle, but it's a more dangerous game now. Today, people who never wanted to play are dying."

"And you can change that?" she said.

"That number is how many died of hypothermia and cold-related illnesses in one country. Each year, they are dying by the hundreds of thousands worldwide, and more die than are counted."

"You're a dad," she said.

"Which is why I'm still talking to you."

"And a husband," she said.

"Never have I felt more like a husband than now," he said.

"And I admire your moral intelligence, always have," she said. "But this is not winnable, and all of the families of your morally intelligent and scientifically brilliant friends are being left to mourn good years they would have had with their brothers and husbands and sons."

"We're living in an Ice Age that started three million years ago, and most people literally cannot understand that," he said. "If more people understood the system's underlying state, they could understand how they have been lied to and manipulated. When you see someone die of hypothermia, the fact that the planet is in an ice age becomes that much clearer. Do you understand?" He thought he was more objective when it came to the perils of cold than most people, but in a way, he was an especially unobjective person. He was starting to get upset now; the death of his colleague Oliver Brown all those years ago, coupled with Micah Ritchie's case of hypothermia in Hawaii, had never stopped obsessing him. He saw a realization appear in her eyes but different from the one he had hoped to produce.

"It's not that you guys came up with this together, is it?" she said. "*You* came up with it, didn't you? You sentenced your friends to death."

"One person doesn't give birth to an idea like this," he said. "You know that from the history of science. People co-invent just about every breakthrough, sometimes at the same time and place and sometimes scattered around the globe."

"This is a breakthrough?" she said.

"I can't talk to you when you're like this," he said.

"You *make* me like this," she said.

"Okay, let's talk later." The sound of little feet came from the hallway into the kitchen.

"Mommy!" said Sarah, their sweet redheaded daughter, age four. She was dragging her security blanket on the floor as she entered her parents' midst.

"Hi, baby," Amy said.

"I called for you a long time."

"I'm sorry I didn't hear, sweetheart," Amy said. "I am glad you are here now. Give me a hug."

10

Whit and the rest had been at Mount Erebus during the Southern Hemisphere summer, in February 2021, with the continual and unforgiving winter darkness of June, July, and August rendering fieldwork out of the question. Mount Erebus was another case where the relationship among geothermal activity, water in all three phases, and the movement of magma meant it gave a cornucopia of data and potential insight. Everyone on the team had earned his slot; talking to colleagues was like talking to a brighter version of oneself, or so it seemed to Whit. It was certainly true when it came to O'Brien but no less when it came to Dema Choedrak, Luigi Corso, and the others. Although Choedrak was not a trained volcanologist or even geologist, his background in atmospheric science and climatology pushed him into the field early in his career. He co-authored several papers in Chinese journals with subglacial volcanology experts, primarily based on his field research into ice-melt vectors in non-volcanic environments. His ability to anticipate ice melt, or the absence of it, on or off a volcano, was unmatched. Choedrak was thrilled that Whit knew how to play Chinese chess and had thought to bring along a set. All but one of the eight researchers on the team were chess players; teaching them the basics of the Chinese version of the game only took a few days, with Whit and Choedrak taking turns as the tutor. The game had idiosyncrasies, to be sure. Most prominent was a river at the center of the board, beyond which some pieces did not move. Another was that soldiers, the equivalent of pawns in Western chess, could move laterally and not just forward once across the river. A third: soldiers could not be traded for pieces once they attained the opponent's back row. Most problematic for newcomers to the game, kings were confined to a square court at the rear of the board and always had to have one piece separating them from the opposing king. In other words, there was no removing the last piece separating your king from your opponent's king, as that would mean your king would be in the same column as your opponent's, face to face, as it were, even though at a distance. It was a subtle rule that took getting used to and was central to achieving checkmate.

The first game played on the expedition was between Choedrak and Whit before anyone had asked to learn.

"It is excellent that you brought this," Choedrak said.

"I love the game," Whit said, making his third move, pushing the rough equivalent of a knight forward one space and diagonally one space.

"Where did you learn?" said Choedrak, pushing his own "knight" forward.

"My parents were at the University of Washington in Seattle, where there were tons of Asian kids. A Chinese friend's dad taught me. Then I would play against the son or the dad whenever I got the chance. When they moved, his dad gave me a board to remember them by."

"Is this it?" Choedrak said.

"This is it," Whit said.

"Cool," Choedrak said. Whit's thoughts turned to an event the day before. He and Michael O'Brien had revealed their true thoughts regarding the Climatists on the heels of a series of elliptical conversations over the previous two years. Admitting to such ideas was ill-advised in most contexts, to the point of being career-ending. Indeed, Whit's parents were two of the first to have their careers ruined by the Climatists. Neither lost their tenured appointments at the University of Washington. However, they had each lost the right to teach classes, their faculty mailboxes, their offices, and, by far the most painful, eye contact from all but an emeritus faculty member or two, who had little to lose by refusing to shame them. It had been awful for the elder Thorgasons and nearly as awful for Whit. Shame showered down on him and his brothers in a community that had once treated the family like low-level celebrities, which they were in the realm of science. When the day before, out on the ice, O'Brien had said that he, too, felt as though he was living in an era of progressively intense anti-science, Whit breathed easily for the first time in years. Neither came remotely close to launching any plan, but they had said important words.

"My brother," O'Brien said.

"Brother," Whit said.

Then they had let the words resound for a few moments. Whit's thoughts returned to the game in front of him and the man he was playing against. He had read a paper of Choedrak's that made him believe Choedrak shared at least some of his and O'Brien's views.

He had decided to find out, though he had to overcome palpable fear just to speak.

"I read your paper about Himalayan climate cycles," Whit said, making his next move on the board.

"And?" Choedrak said, answering with his own move per the traditional opening they were employing. From the start of the game, Whit had the feeling that his skills would not be sufficient to give Choedrak much of a test, but he was nonetheless committed to the fight. Everything around them had an otherworldly orange hue from the midnight sun's lemon-yellow light passing through the red tent. Whit paused before speaking, leaving his hand on the piece he was thinking of moving next. He couldn't decide whether to talk or play first. He spoke.

"And it reminded me of some of the work my parents did," he said. "When did people forget that climate was here before we began measuring it, just doing what it did? When did people forget that the Holocene itself has seen cycles that would flabbergast the average undergrad?"

Next, to change the subject, he moved on the board, trying not to fumble the game and put his career at risk in the same sixty seconds.

"Your parents were good scientists," Choedrak said, with his right hand continuing to follow the opening gambit both knew well. "Or should I say they are good scientists; are they still living?" Whit's eyes closed as he felt some of the ancient hurt.

He made his first creative move in their game. "They are living on retirement income, unable to publish or do much. Things got rough for them. But thank you. No one has told me my parents were good scientists in a long time. You probably know what happened to them at U. of W."

"I did hear something," Choedrak said, considering Whit's move, before deploying a left-flank soldier.

"After their administrative punishment, they still had their official titles, as well as their income," Whit said. "But they couldn't stand being shunned by people who had been friends, so they moved us to Alaska. I was a junior in high school. Since I was already obsessed with glaciers, the move had its advantages. Although, honestly, it had sometimes been easier for me to get to the Cascades glaciers than to get to ones from Anchorage. But these were large glaciers and happened to be much in the news. I could see my career opening up for me, although I still hadn't gotten into college, even as my parents' careers were ending. We agreed I would either pretend to believe in manmade climate change or keep my head down, which I did for as long as possible."

"You cannot destroy courage," Choedrak said.

When Whit looked down, he saw that Choedrak had left a cannon vulnerable in a way that didn't make sense. He took it and then, five moves later, extended his right hand over the board to congratulate Choedrak, who had used the cannon as bait.

"Let's play more later," Choedrak said. "There are things we should talk about without distraction."

"Sure," Whit said.

"With the way the goons are accumulating power, there is not much time for anyone to slow them," Choedrak said.

"No, there isn't," Whit said.

"I am a gentle person," Choedrak said. "This is known about me in my extended family and our community. But I am prepared to do what I can to expose the lies of the Climatists. You have been thinking about this very much. I know this."

"I have ideas," Whit said. "That does not mean that they are good."

"You are a good man," Choedrak said. "That means that at least some of your ideas are good."

"You should talk to my wife about that," Whit said. Choedrak smiled, and Whit continued. "I saw a friend die of hypothermia, and it haunts me. He was another scientist with a team I was on in the Canadian Rockies. I also saw a surfer in Hawaii get hypothermia to the point of being in trouble."

"I am sorry about your friend," Choedrak said.

"The situations in which they got hypothermia could not have been more different," Whit said, "but it killed one of them and could have led the other to drown. One day I was thinking about the global mean temperature and how people think it's skyrocketing because of how it is presented—as an anomaly."

"It is as clever as anything the Climatists have done," Choedrak said.

"As you know, people are dying because of economic responses to the planet's supposedly skyrocketing temperature," Whit said. "So, I was thinking how the Holocene is a pause in the Ice Age that started three million years ago, but the planet is still icier and colder than ideal for most people living farther away from the Equator than a couple of thousand miles. Even with modern clothing, well-constructed habitations, and modern heating systems, we are stalked by cold during half the year."

"You and I agree," Choedrak said, "but I am not clear why you are saying this."

"People don't know this simple fact," Whit said. "They don't know because it has been hidden from them by the extraordinary successes of the second half of the twentieth century."

"And you wish to show them that the world is cold," Choedrak said.

"I'm going to say something that is going to sound crazy," Whit said.

"I am ready," the gray-bearded, brown-eyed Choedrak said, looking at him.

"If people saw a scientist die in a controlled environment kept at Earth's average temperature, it could change some minds."

"That is very crazy," Choedrak said.

"I know," Whit said.

"I am not ready to do that," Choedrak said. "And you, you cannot do that. You are a husband and a father."

They talked about the idea past midnight while fitting in another game.

Choedrak was the one to observe that people ran into burning buildings to save others all the time, with the rescuers dying in the process. No one considered that suicide. If the Climatists could be stopped, millions of lives would be saved.

Whit said that during the Second World War, when soldiers dove on top of hand grenades to save the other men in their unit, they were remembered as heroes. "How is this different?" he said.

When they put away the board and drew their sleeping bags up to their necks, it was 2 A.M., four hours until their alarms would sound. Whit closed his eyes and found himself exhausted and exhilarated in equal measure. Choedrak looked at him in silence, contemplating.

11

Anyone risking their reputation and money by betting that weather will or will not generate disasters on Earth in any five years should always bet that it will. And that is what the Climatists figured out. On the way to this realization, most were trying to serve and protect the public by raising red flags about a potentially unprecedented nexus of problems. But later, quieter research showed that everything that could happen on Earth, in terms of weather and climate, had already happened, anywhere from hundreds to thousands of times.

There were always droughts, floods, tropical cyclones, wildfires, tornadoes, and hailstorms. The only thing new was the professional news crews and cellphone-wielding citizens sending images of each grim swath of destruction around the globe. At casinos, the house always wins; the Climatists, betting on telegenic devastation, became the house. They didn't need anything unprecedented, even though they falsely claimed to bear witness to "unprecedented" phenomena constantly. They only required the repetition of past weather disasters or even a pale approximation of one.

China's Yangtze River flood in 1931 was one example of a horrifying historical disaster. Killing between two and four *million* people, the devastation wrought by the flood was biblical.

The floodwaters performed much of the killing, and disease and starvation (owing to crop failures) did the rest.

The preceding two years, 1928 and 1929, had been a time of extreme drought in China. Then, in the winter of 1930-1931, unusually heavy snowfalls occurred in the Yangtze River basin, priming the system for the flooding that ensued. Rebellions during the same period as the drought had left the Yangtze and associated rivers in poor condition; in times of peace, the rivers were carefully tended to maximize water flow. Agricultural diversions of water channels had left the system less able to pass the volume of water to the sea. With melted snow having left the Yangtze swollen and all the land saturated, tropical cyclones struck China from the south and created the worst flood in memory.

The Yangtze River flood of 1931 was nearly invisible to the bulk of humanity. Even better for the Climatists, they learned they didn't need a Yangtze-scale event, although some hoped for one (to assist them in silencing the last of the skeptics). They could do fine with a flood that was a tenth or even a hundredth its size. So it was that a 2024 flood in Nebraska in which property was lost, livestock drowned, and a few hundred people who refused to evacuate or turn around at flooded crossings lost their lives now passed for biblical in the public imagination. Suppose you argued that drawing a line between Yangtze 1931 and Nebraska 2024, with the assumption that "climate change" was now driving weather disasters. In that case, evidently, such events were becoming dramatically *less catastrophic* than in the early twentieth century, and you were written off as grossly insensitive.

The house always wins.

If someone used a time machine to record crystal-clear video of China's 1931 flood, then and only then would the children of modernity have a lens through which to see their own era clearly. With no onlooker possessing such a machine, the Climatists rode a wave of fear to prominence and, eventually, to the control of media, universities, and governments.

If you were a Climatist, the mid-2020s had been a particularly abundant opportunity to instill fear. Katla's eruption whipped up supposedly unprecedented weather across Europe and, to a lesser extent, the rest of the Northern Hemisphere; sixty-year ocean cycles entering their cold phases had contributed to the most frigid winters that people younger than eighty had lived through. Headline writers feasted on the scenes presented by photographers and reporters around the globe:

EUROPE STILL DIGGING OUT AFTER WORST BLIZZARD IN MEMORY
GREAT LAKES ICY ON FOURTH OF JULY
CROP FAILURES ACROSS CHINA

With the weather, and misperceptions of it, suddenly askew, it didn't matter if it happened before; it mattered that it was happening now. The Climatists had no trouble convincing people that the bitter, life-threatening cold was a symptom of global warming. Some of the last of the publicly identifiable climate heretics had joked among themselves after snowfalls that they were getting tired of shoveling all the global warming. Still, it was the same kind of gallows humor popular in the former Soviet Union during the Cold War. You had to know that the system was rigged against truth to get the joke.

To those paying sustained attention, the 2020s represented a fearful pivot point when fossil fuels were being abandoned at record rates while the need for them was on the verge of exploding. But that was a minority view, and the Climatists

mopped up the rhetorical battlefield while making it their business to frighten the latest generation of children into believing
they were living in end times, all of it due to their parents' (and
grandparents') climate sins.

Not a single opportunity to deepen the public's fear was
wasted. As 720-pixel high-definition video gave way to 1080
pixels, which gave way to 1440 pixels, which gave way to 2160
pixels, fires had never burned so brightly before so many human eyes. Images of disasters had never been disseminated so
widely or so clearly. Meanwhile, worse fires and floods of a century before (and earlier) were unknown. A tornado in Kansas
killed seventy-nine people in 2026; the horrifying event was
videoed by more than a hundred different high-definition cameras. If you mentioned the Tri-State Tornado of 1925 that had
killed *ten times* as many people, there was only one possible reason: You were an ignorant buffoon who didn't care about your
fellow man.

And thus, governments, in the name of bringing back the
imagined fair weather of yesteryear, convinced whole popula-
tions to keep increasing electricity generation from wind and
solar as fast as possible. It rendered utility bills drastically more
expensive and froze people to death in their homes. Meanwhile,
figuring into the dark calculus was the tendency for freezing to
death to be something people did quietly—unlike the clamor
the Climatists made at every move.

Perhaps even more out of view than past weather events was
that the Climatists' "green energy" depended on nightmarish
forms of mining, multiplying hazardous exposures in unfortunate parts of both industrialized and developing nations. The
explosion of new toxicity sprang from the extraction of raw
materials, the production of equipment, and the disposal of

batteries (and other forms of concentrated toxicity). Lithium toxicity was already threatening drinking water in China and elsewhere on an unprecedented scale. Meanwhile, it was impossible to find Climatists willing to acknowledge China's ecological devastation owing to the new practices or any of the other environmental catastrophes midwifed by "green" corporate greed.

II

I don't wanna hear about what the rich are doin'
I don't wanna go to where, where the rich are goin'
They think they're so clever, they think they're so right
But the truth is only known by guttersnipes

—The Clash, "Garageland"
(Songwriters: Joe Strummer and Mick Jones)

12

There was another video awaiting Erica, Ben, and their colleagues. Watching each new recording had become progressively more difficult, at least for some.

A video a week earlier had been that of a seventy-five-year-old guy from Finland: white-bearded Silvestras Jakauskas, whose red t-shirt made him look like Santa Claus. His video was the most rattling yet for Erica and most working on the fourth floor. It started with an aggressive statement:

> The "fact" that ninety-seven percent of all the world's scientists are convinced climate is going crazy and that it's mankind's fault is no fact. No journalist has verified this claim or looked through the academic literature objectively. If they did read it scientifically, they would see that arguments about nearly everything climate-related have never stopped.

After this pronouncement, the elderly Finn had gone through the usual Fifty-Niner routine, dying in a little over thirteen hours. There was something about a guy from a Nordic country resembling Santa Claus perishing in 59-degree air; it stayed with people. Chip Sutcliffe observed a faint destabilizing effect the video had on rival networks and other media outlets; he took special note of murmurings of discontent within the staff of his own show. He also tasked Steve Tripp with fact-checking the Finnish Fifty-Niner's outlandish statement. Tripp was the only one among their team who had studied science in any depth in college and had continued with his reading of peer-reviewed papers on climate ever since. Each time he read a new one, it made him feel worse about humanity's prospects. But without knowing it, Tripp had restricted his diet of articles to those confirming his own well-polished views. For this project, he purposely sought dissent; he inhaled journals, including Chinese, Indian, and Japanese journals. To his faint surprise, Sutcliffe approved his request for budgeted funds to get them translated by a firm whose versions were far cleaner than Google's. Plowing through the dozens of articles, the true breadth of perspectives was clear as day. Just as important: it was undeniable to Tripp that there was little to no consensus about anything climate. Clouds, tropical cyclones, glaciers, floods, droughts, lightning, ocean currents, land use—and the effects that changes in any of them would have on the system—were all being argued about if you had eyes to see.

Ten days into the marathon reading, Sutcliffe asked him what he was finding.

"He was right," Tripp said. "There's more dissent than most think. And in the Asian journals, it's pretty much the wild west. It's fascinating."

"That's not something to broadcast," Sutcliffe said.

"Understood," Tripp said. He had, however, taken the liberty of informing Erica, Ben, and Guzman.

And now there was a new video, which Erica didn't want to watch. Ben had been the first of them to see it. He and Erica were two of the four producers responsible for covering the story of the Fifty-Niners, the other two being Tripp and Guzman. In the past four months, all of them had watched fourteen videos of intelligent, accomplished scientists brimming with life who put themselves in a controlled environment kept at Earth's average temperature and died. The first few took a toll on all of them, but for Erica, whose passion for doing news was framed around global warming, looking at them had become excruciating. For her, it had been easier to watch gruesome videos terrorists sent around the Internet than to watch the Fifty-Niners' last moments of life caught on camera. And with the passing weeks, she had shared the outer edges of her suffering with Ben.

He, too, had been with the climate majority all his adult life, despite coming from an Alabama family whose members included oil people. Barbecues and birthday parties were occasions for ribbing him by a few of the more strident of these when he still lived down south. Yet as the rest of the country became more lockstep around the idea that Armageddon was taking place on their television screens each night as out-of-control weather, he had stopped defending himself. He knew his denier relatives would or wouldn't realize that they were on the wrong side of history, while his conscience was clear. "Never explain yourself," his Uncle Jeb had told him one day as the two floated down the Cahaba River in inner tubes with Bud Lights in their hands and a cooler full of them floating nearby. The uncle and nephew had been talking about Ben's recent breakup and its effect on his mother's mental state. With time, his mother's faith in him was restored. But his Uncle Jeb's three simple words proved the most important advice he ever received. The last of his relatives to taunt him about his climate thoughts before his move north could see in his eyes that the bombs were no longer reaching their target. The burden of figuring out how he would explain himself to them had been lifted, and soon they stopped trying to get under his skin.

His fellow journalists in the South had shared his views on climate, if in a casual way. At NBC up here in New York, though, having strong opinions on the subject was a prerequisite for career advancement and part of the glue that bound people together. Staff members at *The Nightly News* talked about weather events at places they had never been a surprising amount of the time.

For him, the Fifty-Niners' videos were fascinating. He'd watched them with Erica and on a few occasions in the conference room with Sutcliffe and others, but he also had watched them alone. Part of it was that he had trouble digesting the idea that you could die of hypothermia at 59 degrees Fahrenheit, the same temperature people had told him all his life was dangerously high. The scientists in the tapes kept mentioning that the planet was experiencing an Ice Age, which had only been interrupted by a set of lucky circumstances for humanity. That didn't make sense, but it seemed to him that the shivering on the tapes was legitimate, that the thermometers were likely accurate, and that when the scientists' bodies were visible on the floor toward the end of the videos, it was real, too. Seeing someone in shorts and a T-shirt who had just frozen to death was, for some reason, gripping.

He had watched the new video on his own. It featured another geologist, a New Zealander who had never publicly shown a whiff of doubt about the climate narrative before his video. A link to it had been forwarded to Ben by Martin Smith, a news producer in Auckland, with whom Ben had partnered on a project the year before. The message from Smith was characteristically pithy: "Kiwis have joined the hateful club—Martin."

After watching it, Ben had gone to Erica's office, and she'd said the bit about not wanting even to hear of another video.

"You are thoughtful," she said, accepting a latte he'd had his assistant fetch.

"Sometimes," Ben said. "Then again, I brought you another video."

"I'll get over it," she said.

He wheeled a chair from the other side of the desk so he could sit beside her, put his laptop in front of them, and opened it. Then he exhaled.

"Ready?" he said. Erica took a sip before responding. "No," she said.

"Whoever is?" he said, pushing PLAY.

The scene was familiar: a lab room, probably in the bowels of a science building, windowless, but with a man who appeared closer to Ben and Erica's ages than anyone else they had seen in a Fifty-Niner video. He was tan, had thinning, light blond hair, and wore a short-sleeve blue T-shirt with SCIENTIST in white letters across the front, black rugby shorts, and beat-up leather flip-flops. The room was 59 degrees Fahrenheit; fans mimicked conditions on an average spring day in Auckland, a readout at the bottom of the video explained. The temperature readouts were in the familiar places at the top of the screen; the scientist had taken the trouble to display both Celsius and Fahrenheit.

"My name is Bob Rutherford," the man said into the fish-eye camera. He was lanky and athletic, and his accented voice was pleasant and musical. "I am a geologist at the University of Auckland, where I also received my undergraduate and doctoral degrees. I have been pursuing my scientific passion since I was a teenager, but more important than that, I am a loving husband

and son. My wife, parents, and all my closest friends and family know what I am doing today."

"Jesus Christ," Erica said.

"We Fifty-Niners are almost sure to lose in our effort to restore sanity to the world. The forces arrayed against us are more powerful than most everyday people can understand, and we accept this fact. What we do not accept is for science to lose its position as a beacon of truth permanently. And thus, we hope that our acts may one day serve as a trail of crumbs by which our children, grandchildren, or great-grandchildren, if need be, will find their way home to the proud and vital lighthouse that science once was. For, inevitably, there will be some who ask, 'Why would happy and good people give their lives in this way?' It is a good question, the best question. And the answer is there was no other way.

"My family know that by giving my life today, I am honoring the person they loved and the science I loved with the last fuel I have. May our lighthouse burn brightly again."

"Shit, shit, shit," Erica said.

"I can pause it; you can also never watch this," Ben said. Erica reached out and pushed PAUSE herself.

"We've still never seen a body," she said. "They've shuffled off this mortal coil without a journalist being allowed to photograph their body or a doctor to do an autopsy. Maybe they died from hypothermia, and maybe they're all laughing at a bar somewhere."

"You seriously believe the funerals and burials were for empty boxes?" Ben said.

"I do not, no," Erica said. "But for a bunch of people who take proof so seriously, they've been unwilling to provide evidence of what they've done." She pressed PLAY.

"Though my wife is not a scientist, she loves science and says it's one reason she loves me. My wife lost a wonderful person, her great-uncle, who died of what is about to kill me in his own home in 2015. In his seventies, Uncle Kelly was a pensioner with more than a dozen prescriptions keeping him alive. He lived humbly in a small flat in Dunedin but lost out in the survival lottery. The question for him was always: Do I spend what it takes to fill my stomach, to have the medications keeping me alive, or to keep my flat warm? In his case, one of those medications was a blood thinner, which made staying warm harder. With New Zealand having seen its electric prices double and Uncle Kelly's flat being warmed by electricity, it was perhaps inevitable that he would keep adding another layer of wool and turning down the heat a little more. He was found by a neighbor who said his flat was seventeen degrees Celsius, slightly warmer than the room I'm in now.

"It's difficult, let's be clear, to count the number who have died this way. Governments make efforts, but families in the industrialized world are often embarrassed when they lose someone to fuel poverty. Many hide it. Well, as a scientist who is clear about the supposedly unprecedented nature of the climate of this era, it's my job to let the public know when misunderstandings about science are killing them. This is such a time, a strange moment. Never have opinions so skillfully masqueraded as knowledge. May what I am doing today, and what those will do after me, decrease the years that elapse before knowledge holds more power than opinions again, and science is returned to its role as the great hope of humankind." Rutherford's temperature was 98.9 degrees, and his pulse 102. There was a flutter in the video as it played on the laptop, and when the fluttering ended, time had advanced three hours. Rutherford's green-blue eyes were less bright; he remained on the folding chair, but his shivering made it difficult. His temperature was 96.8, and his pulse 125.

"If you're wondering if it's difficult to remain committed to what I'm doing here, the answer's no," he said. "If you're wondering if it's painful, the answer's yes." At the six-hour point, perhaps concerned he'd slur his words, he held a piece of printer paper with "STILL HURTS" written in green block letters. His body temperature was 95; his pulse 115. He'd suppressed his shivering to hold up the sign, but he only managed for a short while. When the shaking overwhelmed his intention, half a piece of paper was in each of his hands.

At nine hours, he had climbed on the lab table behind his folding chair and laid on the table's black surface in the fetal position, thumb in mouth.

"There is only so much I can deal with," Erica said, prompting Ben to push PAUSE.

"Enough?" he said.

"I want to finish watching because it's my job," she said. "I just never thought my career would force me to deal with evil like this." Ben gave a quizzical look.

"You've done stories on African warlords," he said.

"Most of those warlords knew they were evil, living in an evil world," she said. "These guys think they're good, living in a world on the edge of darkness. I just can't stand the misplaced self-righteousness. Am I wrong to think it's evil?"

"You're not wrong," Ben said.

The paused video showed Rutherford's temperature to be 92 degrees and his heart rate to be 73.

The New Zealander proved himself a winner at twelve hours: fastest to die. He was face-down on the lab table, head turned toward the camera, a puddle of drool next to his cheek.

"Why do some die fast and others slow?" Erica asked.

"Scientists know a good amount about hypothermia, but the way it unfolds in each case is almost completely unpredictable," Ben said.

"WebMD?" Erica said.

"Give me more credit than that," Ben said.

"No, really," Erica said.

"Let's just say that Google Scholar and I are well acquainted."

"Okay, no one's doubting your skills," Erica said. "Basically, we'll never know why this guy died first?"

"Pretty much," Ben said.

There was a knock. Guzman and Tripp stood in the doorway.

"Come in," Erica said. The new arrivals grabbed extra chairs, wheeled them in front of Erica's desk, and sat.

"You saw it?" Ben said.

"Yeah," Guzman said.

"At least he died quick," Tripp said, "less to watch."

"How much of what he said did you believe he sincerely meant?" Erica said.

"Does that matter?" Guzman said. "Chip wants a panel of scientists for tonight."

"Well, I take your point that it might not matter for the broadcast," Erica said, "but I was asking, just personally, who thinks these people believe what they're saying?"

"That's the thing, dear," Guzman said. "Climate's not about belief; it's about facts. And the fact is that ninety-seven percent of scientists say the climate is in crisis, which means you're in crisis, and I'm in crisis, and these losers on the videotapes are distracting the world from the things that need to be done to contend with that."

"The thing is, I believe they're sincere, unfortunately," Erica said. "This guy's family green-lighting him to be a Fifty-Niner pushed me over the edge."

"I don't believe a word they're saying," Guzman said. "But that's neither here nor there. We need scientists for tonight."

"So, the basic idea is they're going to come on the air to say Santa Claus was wrong?" Erica said. Finnish scientist Jakauskas's video the week before was the last one most people had seen. It had done a lot of damage.

"Pretty much," Tripp said. "The best climatologists in the country know he was deceived, at best. Three willing to go on-air shouldn't be a problem."

And it hadn't been. Chosen were a scientist from Columbia University (seventy blocks uptown from Rockefeller Center), one from NASA (which had its own climatologists on the Columbia campus), and one from Rutgers. The three stated that Fifty-Niners were mentally ill, by definition, and should be pitied and not emulated. As for the science, each insisted that the fact humankind was facing a crisis of its own making was something about which there was no more uncertainty than about gravity itself.

13

It turned out Juanita missed Michael even more than she thought she would. During their long affair, she had lived without him more than ninety percent of the time, not much more than she was living without him now. But being unable to look forward to the next visit made her stomach clench.

He had proved himself a romantic, sending dozens of postcards over the years, including some from their vacations. Juanita had appreciated the spy-like gesture of his managing to buy, write, stamp, and send the cards while she shopped, slept, or showered—or whenever he managed to achieve these small coups. Now that he was gone, these were the ones that meant the most. Partly, it was the fact that, despite the strange shape of their union, they made it clear how crazy he was about her. Not that she didn't appreciate the ones sent from the places his work brought him where she hadn't been able to join him. Indeed, she read and reread all the cards in the first weeks after he was gone.

Sometimes tears came; usually, they didn't. On a few occasions, holding one in her hands and reading it in candlelight, it felt like Miguel was in the room with her. But she wasn't reading them to cry; she read them to be with him.

Although he favored postcards, he had also managed to send a small number of letters, most with photographs of the volcano he was working on at the time. Even long after the world had gone digital, his formal letters and accompanying paper photographs continued. The images were beautiful. Juanita had appreciated them when they came, but now in his forever absence, they were like oxygen.

His connection to nature was strong, and the photos showed the relationship well. They had helped him to document his work but also to appreciate it, he'd told her, adding that when taking the pictures that excited him the most, he was thinking of her when he pressed the shutter button. She had been his muse, his audience, and his closest friend rolled into one.

After his death, she painted canvases based on Miguel's pictures, completing five in different sizes in just two months. As she had with his portrait, she added his first name, in English, to each one. She had based two on photos of the Chilean volcano Calbuco, where he had done research and which had drawn him toward her before they met, so many years before. One painting was of Mount Rainier, and two were of Klyuchevskoy, a glacier-crowned volcano in Kamchatka. As she had with the portrait of him later brought down on her head by the enraged Climatist, she posted photos of the paintings on social media. She knew that most judged her for defending her Fifty-Niner boyfriend and imagined she was joining the climate fight in his place. She wasn't. She was simply unwilling for so many people who never knew the man she knew him to be to imagine they had the right to try, judge, and condemn him in absentia the way so many had. They could have all the feelings they wanted to about climate, but when it came down to shaming the love of her life, that was a different matter.

As a painter and a person who loved nature, she found the photographs of the volcanoes worthy of her attention. Miguel's eye was exceptional for that of a non-artist, and many of the shots captured a day's first or last light as it played on the frozen nooks of the volcanoes transcendently.

She had dozens of photographs from which to choose for her next, sixth painting and had come close to selecting one of Katla. He had gotten good shots of several significant explosive eruptions by leaving reinforced cameras on-site and retrieving them after the events had played out. One was of Katla. She and Miguel had looked at it more than once, and she decided, looking at it now, that it would be her subject.

Miguel's love of volcanoes hadn't stemmed just from a boyish interest in eruptions; the highly cerebral science constructed around their existence had reeled him in no less. But the fact that volcanoes were uncontrollable natural forces did captivate him, of course, and it was something he talked about when they were together. Looking at the image from the Katla eruption, she felt a great pang, remembering Miguel and the world they had shared.

It was 11:30 P.M. when she decided to use the photo of Katla starting the following morning. She got herself ready for bed, left the picture on her nightstand, set her alarm for 6:30, and fell asleep. When her alarm sounded, she felt a chill in the apartment. It was May in Concepción, a month before the winter solstice; Juanita pulled on jeans, a sweater, and thick socks. Then she finished a glass of water she found on her dresser, picked up the photograph, and went to the kitchen to put on the kettle.

She had set a canvas on the easel the night before. She walked nearly the length of the loft to her painting station with the photo and her coffee. She clipped the picture to the easel, pulled a hairband from her wrist, put her almost black hair in a ponytail, and took a sip of strong coffee. The more artsy shots taken by Miguel she'd started with had been satisfying to paint. Looking at the image of Katla during its explosive eruption, she felt her heart beating in a way it hadn't in a long time.

There was much to capture here: the violent upward motion of ash, rocks, dust, and steam. But there was also just the fact that Katla was done resting. People the world over might be drowning in television, smartphones, computers, and social media, but Katla was done resting. The fact of the occurrence and of nature's power was mesmerizing.

Using charcoal pencils, she had sketched the glaciers and volcanoes themselves first for previous eruption works. Unlike Calbuco in her own country and Klyuchevskoy in Kamchatka, both cones that fit well with most people's ideas of what a volcano looked like, Katla was a nondescript mountaintop that appeared, from some perspectives, almost flat. The apparent form was a trick played by Mýrdalsjökull glacier sitting on it like a giant white pancake, cloaking Katla's subtle conical shape. When she felt she had Katla in a form that made sense, she turned to the eruption.

She started with a series of lines showing cracks in the glacier. Then she outlined the massive quantity of material surging upward from the caldera, followed by the small amounts of ejecta showering down. She estimated that sketching and painting would take at least fifty hours. Never had she painted an image that showed so much movement. The feeling that Miguel was with her returned. If she could go back in time and tell him she found volcanoes as obsessively fascinating as he did, she would. The best she could do, absent a time machine, was to paint with her heart beating in its insistent, electrifying way, ten and twelve hours a day for the next four days.

When she finally added his name, it came as a great relief. She set down her brush and cried without restraint.

14

Surprisingly, the idea came to Erica when she was tucking in her daughters for the night. With blonde Sarah five and brown-haired Monica almost nine, sharing a room as they still did would likely become unworkable soon. Meanwhile, the two girls were close and would have likely both chosen to share a room, even if offered the chance to have their own. The family just managed to afford the two-bedroom co-op on the East Side, which made both Erica's and her husband's commutes workable, and she worried about where the transition to a less confining space might take them. Connecticut, Westchester (where she'd grown up), Queens, and Long Island sounded equally foreign and less than ideal. Sarah sighed when she got her kiss, as though a good day had just ended well. Monica was sleepy, too, but not as near unconsciousness as her sister.

"Are you going to be late tomorrow?" Monica asked as she received her kiss.

"Probably, honey. It has been a hard few months, I know."

"It's okay; I know you're here when you can be."

"You're right about that," Erica said, "and I always will be. Night-night."

"Night, Mommy."

It suddenly occurred to Erica that neither she nor her children had known one cold moment in their East 82nd Street apartment.

Though she was enough of a New Yorker to be able to use the transit system without blinking, if need be, she knew the days when she made use of it were essentially over. Ubers and yellow taxis got her to work, and Lincoln Town Cars, provided by the company, conveyed her home. The nanny did the bulk of the family's grocery shopping. Erica's own reasons to go outside were few, and the opportunities to do it, even when she would have wanted, were fewer still. She hadn't even been in Central Park, on foot, in over a year, and it made her feel like a terrible parent because that meant she hadn't accompanied her kids to the park during the same stretch. She had experienced similar bouts of guilt innumerable times. But what was new tonight was the understanding that she had become somewhat shockingly insulated from the elements. She knew that people in fly-over country thought this about New Yorkers, and when she was young and unmarried and still in-line skating through the park and doing other things outside, she considered herself living proof that they were all wrong. In fact, she saw what she used to disprove with her own example she now proved in a humbling fashion.

And that's when the inspiration came: She wanted to feel some of what the Fifty-Niners felt. She didn't want to be one of them, not even close. She just wanted to feel what it felt like to be in a room that wasn't, strictly speaking, comfortable. And which was, as they insisted, at the planet's average temperature. She wanted to recreate the same circumstances, see what it was like, and possibly have one of her reporters do a piece about experiencing the same thing. She wasn't sure how it would play out, but she knew she would let herself get colder than she had in a long time.

Her first thought was to run the idea by her husband, but when she got to bed, he was asleep. She kissed him on the forehead, circled to her own side of the bed, climbed in, and fell asleep herself in what felt like seconds.

Upon awakening, her first thought was that she would need to run the idea past Ben, who would likely give her grief. But the sooner she broached it, the sooner she could get to the other side of his disapproval, and Erica was going to need to get there; she was going to need his help.

She approached Ben after their production meeting on Wednesday. "Time for a coffee?" she said.

"Quick one," he said. "We're running Casey's piece on China, and it needs fixes."

"Five minutes," she said.

"I've got that," he said.

It was 10:45 A.M., non-peak hours, which meant they could grab a commissary booth without fear of an aggressive, tray-carrying gang demanding space.

"What's up?" Ben said.

"You know I've come to believe that the Fifty-Niners are sincere."

"You said that," he said. "Does it really matter?"

"Probably not," she said, "but I want to spend a little time in a fifty-nine-degree room, in shorts and flip-flops, with fans pointed at me."

"Feeling suicidal?" he said.

"No, but I'd like to know how much suffering they go through," she said. "Haven't you wondered?"

"Maybe, but I'm guessing I'm less curious about it than you."

"Does your brother still have his lab?" she asked.

"Yeah, why?"

"I'd like to feel a little of what they feel, not just the cold."

"That's not going to happen," he said.

"Why not?"

"Because my brother does *science* in his lab, has a *career* in his lab," he said. "It's not a make-believe science place for crazed journalists."

"I'm not doing make-believe," she said.

"No?"

"I'm reporting, and you should understand it matters if these guys are acting tough on their videos when they're not suffering at all."

"I'm going to go out on a limb and say it's not fun to freeze to death."

"Fine, but guessing's not good enough," she said. "Will you help me or not?"

"You know that small conference room on the eighteenth floor?" he said.

"Go on," she said.

"It's just about never used," he said. "I'm not sure why they don't convert it to offices."

"Could you get me in there on Saturday?"

"I can get you in there *today*, and so can you," he said. "It's just your ID pass and a combination—three, one, five."

"Has to be Saturday morning," she said. "Can you set the thermostat Friday night? Does it have one? They're rare these days."

"It probably does," he said. "It's a space no one thinks of."

"Can you check the thermostat for me?" she said.

"Sure."

"Can you come with me on Saturday?" she said.

"Probably I can," he said. "I think so; I'll text you."

She was on her way to work Thursday morning when his text came: "conference room thermostat works … Jill says Sat. fine."

As for Keith, her husband, he had made his peace with the long hours associated with the Fifty-Niners' doings when the videos had started. Like his wife, he considered it important to expose these supposed scientists' ruse to confuse, distract, and take advantage of the public for what it was. The children would complain, but she would make it up to them with an extra-special Saturday night.

She texted Ben back as her Uber SUV dropped her at Rockefeller Center: "Thank Jill for me."

Though they had secured permission from spouses to do something work-related that might make a difference in this gigantic story, the plan for Saturday was nonetheless the biggest secret Erica and Ben had kept from their partners in a long time.

For her, the forty-eight hours passed with painful slowness. She immersed herself in a cascade of production work to help make the hours pass, and she also took time to research a quality thermometer to measure the temperature of the conference room. She went with the Thomas Scientific thermometer, ordering two on Amazon. Though she owned plenty of flip-flops, shorts, and T-shirts that she mainly used at the family's summer share, she had Amazon send new ones so as not to be seen packing strange items for a weekend morning work session. Finally, in addition to the room thermometers, there were a pair of scanning thermometers for measuring her body temperature. The total for the order, including next-day delivery, was steep; she put it on her corporate VISA. She felt like she used to during the run-up to Christmas as a child.

Friday proved to be a slow news day—in terms of the Big Three subjects for the show: weather, politics, and the various forms of violence in the world—but she had a story about a burst dam in India to bring to completion; her team had been working on it since Tuesday. The story was so pressing that she got a pass to skip the morning meeting, and at one o'clock, she got a text message from Chip saying the dam story would lead that night. Erica had produced stories that led the broadcast many times in the past, but it was an honor, and a roller-coaster ride, whenever it happened. At 2:15, when she had forgotten for a short time what would be taking place the next day, she got a text from Ben: "I set the thermostat at 59 last night, room freezing this morning... set it to 70 for the day in case anyone goes in but will re-set tonight. Congrats on India."

She dashed off a response before returning to the task at hand: "See you 730 tomorrow . . . thanks for all." The dam failure, leading to the death of more than two hundred people, was not, strictly speaking, a story about climate change. The earthen dam was flagged for maintenance a decade earlier, a fact mentioned in the report. Nonetheless, heavy rains had preceded the failure, and, by this point, images of floodwaters and a few choice modifiers about the precipitation and the water itself—"extremely," "unusual," "out-of-control," and "raging"—were all that was needed to transform a story about corruption into one about climate change. In a world dominated by Climatism, such stories wrote themselves.

She received a few high-fives as she left the newsroom, grabbed the duffel with the new things from her office, and scooted home.

A second glass of red wine after dinner and one ten-milligram melatonin gave her sound sleep, so much so that she was momentarily confused when her phone alarm woke her at 6 A.M. Reaching for her phone, it came to her; she was about to get cold for the first time in a long time. She kissed Keith, fending off his half-kidding effort to pull her into his arms, kissed both girls, who were sleeping soundly, and took the empty elevator down to the lobby, her heart beating in her chest like it had her first day at the job. She had been too preoccupied of late to pay attention to the weather forecast. Stepping from the foyer to pause under her building's awning, she saw that it was a cool morning for May, bright and beautiful. She gave the slightest nod to the Uber driver waiting at the curb, climbed in the backseat, and settled into her thoughts for the ten-minute ride. Although she and Ben weren't to meet for another hour, she had been nervous about the faint possibility of traffic. "If you're not early, you're late" was an expression she made a point of living on the right side of, but sometimes it meant you were left with time on your hands the way she was now. She stepped into a café in the lobby, ordered a caffè macchiato and a blueberry muffin, and sat down with her iPad and breakfast for some more research into the bizarre characters she was about to emulate.

She confirmed that among them, not one had an ex-wife, a colleague, a therapist, or anyone who had come forward to say that their Fifty-Niner's mental health hadn't been all that great. What you got when you dug was that the person was earnest, intelligent, loved nature, and loved science just as much. Absent the fact that they had collectively changed the world conversation about climate change, something that appeared impossible only a few months before, they were a dull lot. They were well-adjusted, hard-working, practical, and optimistic. If you tried, you couldn't have found a less likely group of ideological purists. She looked up their images on Google for about the tenth time in the past week; one by one, she looked into their eyes. There was no rage or maniacal certainty. They were just people who happened to be scientists until the moment they became Fifty-Niners. Scanning their photos with her coffee in hand, it all remained incredible to her, no less than on the day the first video arrived.

At 7:10, she cleaned her table, walked to the elevator, ran her ID through the scanner, acknowledged the guard, and climbed into her second empty elevator car. She found a handicapped bathroom on the eighteenth floor and locked the door behind her. It was clear no one had used the space since the night cleaners had been in if anyone had in the past week. She put the duffel bag on the floor, opened it, and stepped onto her new flip-flops as a tiny changing platform. She changed out of her jeans and into the "Rhododendron Blue" drawstring shorts she'd chosen for herself, took off her Syracuse hooded sweatshirt and replaced it with a gray T-shirt with a pink whale insignia, then wiggled her toes into the flip-flop straps. After zipping the bag closed with the old clothing, she washed her hands, looking at her reflection. It was reassuring to see that, so far as the mirror was concerned, she was just Erica, the girl from Rye with a lot going for her. But there was no getting around the fact that she was pasty white and wearing beach clothing to spend the morning in a conference room flirting with hypothermia, all of which made her feel about as crazy as she could remember feeling. She checked her watch and saw it was 7:25. She got to the conference room one minute later and noticed that lights were illuminating the frosted windows on both sides of the door from within. Ben was waiting there, or the mission was about to be aborted. Erica felt her heart freeze nervously. She inserted her ID card in the reader, saw the light flash green, and entered the combination Ben had told her. Just before the lock would or would not confirm she had the right combination, the door opened from the inside. It was Ben, wearing a beanie and ski parka and flashing a smile.

"You're looking beachy," he said.

"Thank you," she said, "for all this." She put her duffel bag on the conference room table and noted a huge canvas tote of Ben's she had never seen.

"The temperature is right, according to that thermostat," he said.

"I've got four thermometers, two for the air and two for my body," she said.

"We're taking your temperature?" he said. "I thought this was just to feel what it's like to be in a fifty-nine-degree room for a little while."

"It is—mostly," she said. "But I need to go through at least a little of what they've gone through. So"—she lifted the hospital thermometers out of the duffel—"I need to get my temperature down a little. It's chilly in here."

"Fifty-nine degrees isn't that bad, but with the fans blowing on you, you're probably not going to feel great."

"Okay, let me double-check the temperature with these, just to be sure," she said. After asking her husband to put down the girls the night before, she had unwrapped the thermometers in her kitchen, fitting in their batteries before the melatonin took effect. Now she pulled them from the duffel bag, starting with the two air thermometers, pressing their power buttons, and then setting them down.

"Fifty-nine-point-three, same for both," she said.

"Okay, and what about yourself?" he said.

She picked up one of the scanning thermometers, pressed its power button, scanned her forehead, and then held it at arm's length to look at the number.

"Fans?" he said.

"Got 'em," Erica said. "Ninety-eight point three . . . my normal."

"I had you covered if you forgot," he said, patting the side of the tote bag.

"Thank you!" she said.

"You've been busy, so I thought just in case."

"That was very kind," she said.

Ben ran an extension cord to a strip he'd put on the table. He plugged in her fans, which she'd taken out, and turned them on.

"Are we having fun yet?" he asked.

"Kind of," she said. Over his shoulder, she saw a folding chair in the corner of the room nearest the door.

"Was that there, or did you bring it?"

"The latter," he said.

"You were always good," she said.

She checked her wristwatch.

"It's 7:32," she said. "I'm planning to be in here for about two hours."

"Okay," he said. "I should be fine in what I'm wearing."

"That's the thing," she said. "Your being ready to hang out in a cold room is gratefully noted. But I need to get my head as close as possible to where these guys' heads were, and they were each alone for their final hours."

"Sounds creepy, to be honest," Ben said. "Are you sure?"

"I'm sure," she said. "I'll text you when I've had enough."

"I'm going to be in the park," he said.

"Tell the beautiful morning I say hi," she said.

15

While Whit had yet to wear in public a T-shirt adorned with one of the images painted by Mike's Chilean girl-friend, he had paid to have three of them made. He put them on when everyone was asleep. Amy had caught him in one twice, the second occasion at ten o'clock on a Wednesday night in May, a school night, and when she saw him wearing the shirt in the upstairs hallway, on his way to brush his teeth and come to bed, she walked up to him, touched his arm with her hand, and said: "We still need to talk."

"Okay, sure, downstairs?" he said.

"Yup, see you in the kitchen," she said.

So, he turned around, crept down the stairs to prevent creaking that could wake the kids, and made his way to the kitchen for what seemed likely to be a difficult conversation. He felt tempted to tell her about the PR guy he'd heard about on a plane ride, whom he considered the most influential among many powerful people who happened to be Climatists, but there was enough to get through without it.

He threw on a fleece and his slippers; he'd already put the heat down for the night. He put on a kettle and heard her following him down the stairs. "Tea?" he asked as she came in.

"Chamomile, please."

"I'm not leaving you guys behind," he said. "I wouldn't do that."

"I believe you, but not doing further damage isn't good enough," she said. "People have died. I'm sure more are planning to die . . . right?"

"Yeah," he said, finishing their tea.

"Not dying is not good enough," she said. "It doesn't matter if you are morally on the right side of this; you're still on the wrong side of history. No one will remember this stunt except as a speed bump in the last miles before decarbonization."

"Decarbonization is death," he said.

"It is what it is," she said, trying not to sound heartless.

"It's death, not the idea of death or something like death," he said. "It's death for millions before everything is said and done. Do you know how many people have died from hurricanes since they got going with their decarbonization policies?"

"Is that my cue to act as obsessed with this as you are?" she asked.

"Fewer than thirty thousand—over two decades," he said. "Half that many people die yearly because of decarbonization in the United Kingdom alone. It's a silent holocaust. Here," he said, handing her the tea he had made for her. "I get that our children losing their dad and you losing your husband does not make any of that go away, or any of it better. But you've got to understand that we are fighting for the survival of millions of people. It's not just an idea."

"You've lost, Whit," she said. "You'd lost before you started, not because you're a loser. History's unfair; life's unfair; the world's unfair. It's something to accept."

"I'm as much a realist as you," he said, "if not more. You have me over a barrel with this, and you're relishing it." He grabbed his mug and sat on the sofa, leaving a patch of soft green upholstery between them.

"I married a proud man, one with a bright future," she said. "I'm not relishing anything. If I could make this world one where your ideas flourished, I would."

"I'm prepared to let everyone know I'm no longer an organizer or involved," he said. "Will that do?"

"The fact that you were involved will come out," she said. "Do you want your kids to live with the ridicule they'll suffer? You know a little of what that's like. But I'm not sure you know what that would be like in 2028. They're children."

"What would you have me do?" he said.

"I would have you make your own video, in which you explain why you and Mike and the rest of you thought this up," she said. "Then I'd have you tell everyone you've decided any more Fifty-Niners making videos would be a tragic waste of human life."

"Should I throw in that I think the weather has gone crazy, and we only have ourselves to blame?" he said.

"You'd probably be helping your kids if you did," she said. "But I don't expect you to."

"Should I say all the people dying because of fuel poverty should stop doing so as soon as possible because it's really very rude and unsightly?" he said. "Should I say the little people should accept their elite brothers and sisters plunging them into cold darkness so those same elites could assuage the free-floating guilt they feel over not going to church?"

"Funny," she said. "Your altruism, or whatever you want to call it, is leaving a long-lasting stain on this family. And, again, not because it's fair; because it's not fair. But it is so. I need you to care more about your kids' reality than an idea, no matter how noble the idea might be."

"I haven't heard you talk this way," he said. "You've known my thoughts on climate from the start."

"When we were dating, your thoughts weren't killing people," she said. "When we were dating, I didn't know you wouldn't be able to let this go, eventually. When it became clear the Climatists were only going to grow stronger, it seemed only reasonable that you would let go of this fight and move on to the next one."

"There are no other fights with as many people's lives in the balance," he said. "The whole world has it backward about where the threat comes from. I've tried to let it go, but I never told you I was trying to let it go—because I didn't even come close to succeeding."

"Well, now's as good a time as any," she said.

"Have you listened to your grampa's stories about what his brother, your great-uncle, did in Vietnam?" he asked.

"What about them?" she said.

"No, seriously, have you sat down with your grandfather and asked him to tell the stories all the way through?"

"I'm not the biggest war girl; you know that about me."

"He jumped on a grenade, your great-uncle, to save the members of his unit."

"I've heard the story," she said.

"I'm not asking to jump on a grenade," he said. "But you've made me realize one thing. I can't let go of this fight, and you shouldn't want our children's dad to let go of this fight."

"Do you truly think you have a chance of saving a single person by letting this play out?" she said. "Just about the only scientists who have stood up and said they support what you are doing are retired. And, unfortunately, they all look a little nutty if you ask me."

"First, it's important there are some supporting us who lacked the courage to do so before," he said. "Second, climate skeptics have always tended to be in the twilight of their careers, for obvious reasons. You used to act like you were really pissed about what happened to my folks at U.W."

"I was pissed, and I am pissed," she said. "This is not about them. Or maybe it is. Are you trying to retroactively save them? Is that what's happening?"

"I'm trying to save people from freezing to death in their homes because upper-middle-class assholes want to feel self-satisfied about how expensive they've made energy," he said.

"You can't undo what happened to your parents," she said.

"Do you literally not care about fuel poverty?" he said. "I knew I was taking a risk marrying someone a class level above my own."

"Oh, yes, we have a long-standing tradition in my family of eating the poor," she said.

"Well, I'm sorry, but class does matter in this," he said. "You haven't once in your life been told that groceries were going to be a little limited this month."

"Oh, God, please, not the tragic groceries story again," she said.

"We weren't starving to death, fine. But food insecurity and heat insecurity are real, and they worsen each other. I know you care. I know you're fighting off your mama-bear feelings about people other than your children. I know you have them."

"Not in this case," she said.

"I know I can't save the world," he said, "but I can't not try."

"I know," she said.

"I'm not going to be a Fifty-Niner, but I'm proud of the scientists who have, and I'm proud of those who will."

"I basically hate you," she said.

"I know," he said.

But both knew she didn't.

16

It was hard for Erica to tell whether the space felt cold once Ben had left the conference room. The breeze from the fans, set at three different angles so that they were all hitting another part of her while she sat in the chair, was the most uncomfortable thing. The fans were at their lowest setting, just as in the videos. It occurred to her that without them, you could probably last much longer at this temperature without developing hypothermia, let alone dying from it. But she concurred with the Fifty-Niners that if you try to duplicate average conditions on the planet, that should include a moderate amount of wind.

Laptops and tablets, she knew, both gave off heat, so she had ruled against bringing either one with her to make the time pass. She assumed that phones gave off heat, too, however minimal. To prevent being warmed even a tiny amount by her phone, she decided to read books and magazines, as she did on flights work sometimes required, rather than hold her phone in her hands.

She had brought copies of *People*, *Harper's*, and *The New Yorker*, as well as a novel she'd read repeatedly during times of stress. While reading an article in *People* about the British royals, she saw the skin on her legs had goosebumps. As she finished it, she purposefully looked at the skin on her arms and saw that there, too, goosebumps were showing. *That makes sense*, she thought.

The fans are like a breeze on a summer day at the beach. She went back to considering the possibilities of a succession fight in the United Kingdom as they were enumerated by the writer. It was actually fascinating. She checked her watch: 7:58 A.M.

Forerunners of shivering began to assert themselves. By 8:15, Erica felt the first ache of cold in her feet. She had never been able to tolerate it; it meant that time would pass more slowly than it would have. While the awareness of her feet began to sink in, Erica realized her hands also hurt from the cold. For some reason, she had pictured getting cold as something that would take place in her torso and her arms and legs. This was annoying.

The cold in her hands and feet and the shivering she was still just managing to repress made it hard to stay seated. It turned out that the body sends a stream of messages about reversing the trend toward cold. Her mind might be interested in what the Fifty-Niners had experienced, but her body wanted nothing to do with this experiment. *Hey, dumb-dumb, get up, it told her.* She reopened the magazine, but it was clear when she read the same paragraph a few times that the window for passing minutes in that way had closed. She tossed it on the table behind her without caring how it landed. She had to repress the urge to hug herself or keep her elbows against her ribs and her forearms across her abdomen. She had to fight against letting herself cross her legs so that they would warm each other. She had to summon the force of will not to scissor her knees in and out, which she naturally did out of nervousness when writing scripts, but also to warm herself in the office when the air conditioning was blasting.

Ever deepening was the throbbing in her hands and feet. She checked her watch and saw the bad news: she had only passed fifty-seven minutes. She told herself she wasn't really that cold.

She had the impression she had felt once before waiting for a solar eclipse to start. The early stage of the event had been so subtle that you endlessly doubted if it had really begun. Even when the moon had covered nearly half the sun, she had kept wondering, *Is this it?* She was no longer confused about whether her body was trying to shiver; it was. She could still just manage to quell it.

She hadn't been to church since learning her brother had been abused by not one but two priests, and she was surprised now to hear herself repeating the Hail Mary. She whispered it though no one was present who could hear. She remembered her grandmother mouthing the prayer in her kitchen when she thought no one was nearby. It had made an impression on her at the time, but only at this moment was she learning how deep the memory ran. Halfway through her second recitation, she saw she had started scissoring her knees again. She had no idea how long it had been going on and commanded her legs to stop. They did so, but she could see they were biding time for her to become distracted again. Her phone made its text-notification sound on the conference room table; at the same time, her fitness watch vibrated. Picking up the phone, she registered that it was cold to the touch and that the text was from Ben. "How's the Inuit life?" the message read.

"Less cold than you imagine," she texted. Soon, they were messaging back and forth:

BEN: really?
ERICA: really
BEN: that's good
ERICA: yes, and no
BEN: you want suffering?

ERICA: yes and no

BEN: I'm at park ... you should wrap up there ... we should both go enjoy day with families

ERICA: I need at least another hour ... I can get these fans back to you later... don't feel stuck

BEN: I don't ... I feel responsible

ERICA: I'm fine

BEN: seriously, how cold are you?

ERICA: seriously, not very ... not shivering

BEN: I'll text again in an hour

ERICA: You don't have to, but OK

She found his helpfulness stressful, in a way it had never been. Freed from his meddling, she noted that the pain in her hands and feet was reasserting itself. She realized as her attention was brought back to her body that she had told at least one lie while texting with Ben. She would be shivering if she weren't fighting it, and she had distinctly given him the opposite impression.

She put down the phone and realized she was passing through a wormhole into a realm where her discomfort was nearly all she could think of. Beyond her painful hands and feet, there was a sense in her gut that this was a more critical situation than she had anticipated. Another new development: goosebumps up and down her arms and legs had become tiny hubs of pain. There was, too, she suddenly realized, a minor disorientation hovering over everything. She thought to take her temperature but reasoned that if it was still close to normal, she would feel disappointment, and if it was lower than seemed safe, it might encourage her to give up before she had accomplished much.

So, she sat, like an actual Fifty-Niner—no electronics, no book, and not much in the way of thoughts, at least not anything resembling normal ones. She had the urge to get up and make herself hot tea, although she was far from home and from the Keurig on the fourth floor with which she'd made herself teas before she had assistants. It turned out that the brain both received and produced cold-related messages constantly when your temperature started to descend. A wave of regret that she hadn't been close enough to nature to get cold in a long time overwhelmed her. It turned out that feeling this way from time to time was part of being human.

She checked her watch—8:53 A.M.—twenty minutes since her text exchange with Ben. The thought of her best work friend suddenly made her uncomfortable. He was going to try to get her to end this before she wanted; he was sure of it. Meanwhile, she was slightly unclear about how far she wanted to let this research mission go. She didn't want to put herself in harm's way, but she felt driven to bring complete seriousness to what she was doing.

She would take her temperature at nine to see how things were progressing. That meant she had a little more than five minutes to sit. Although she once meditated daily, the practice had fallen by the wayside during the courtship with her husband. Very rarely, mostly in hotel rooms on the road, she still did it, seated in a straight-backed chair for five to fifteen minutes. Overwhelming distractions were all around her and within her, but meditating would make the time pass. She started counting inhalations and exhalations, counting "one" as she inhaled and again on the exhalation. She knew from practice that thirty inhalations and exhalations equaled five minutes. When she was done with the thirtieth breath and checked her watch, it was precisely nine.

She pressed the ON button on the thermometer and held it in

front of her forehead until it beeped. It said her temperature was 97.7 degrees, which was good and bad. It was good because it was the lowest she had seen her temperature and meant the experiment was progressing reasonably, despite the slightly out-of-control nature of her thoughts and feelings. And it was bad because she was starting to feel pretty cold and expected a lower number.

Knowing she would be annoyed waiting for Ben's text at 9:30, she launched a preemptive strike:

ERICA: go be with your fam
BEN: I'm not comfortable leaving you
ERICA: I'm being careful ... hard to concentrate worrying about you wasting a day
BEN: Then get out
ERICA: I'm serious
BEN: I know ... what's your temp?
ERICA: 97.7 as of 9:00 a.m.
BEN: chilly yet?
ERICA: little bit, but the cold's less aggressive than I thought
BEN: your thinking is going to start to get compromised
ERICA: I'm clear-headed
BEN: I'll head home, but I'm going to be texting
ERICA: no, I need to experience the isolation
BEN: you seemed so normal when I met you
ERICA: still normal ... it's called research
BEN: there are more normal kinds of research
ERICA: I'll text you from home after lunch
BEN: I'll live with it
ERICA: thank you

She set down her phone again. She had placed herself behind the table to face the door. So far, it had mercifully stayed closed; she just hoped it would stay that way. When she let her thoughts drift, even to how she would respond if someone came in the room, the shivering rose to the surface and threatened to take over. She decided she would try meditating again but found that her thoughts were racing impossibly. Rather than let them run to whatever bizarre places they might want to carry her, she chose to try something new: staring at the table. It wasn't meditation as she had been taught, but it was something to do while she competed with the urge to let her body start shaking.

The first thing all day that had truly scared her was a sense of well-being she realized was coming over her. It must have happened after she last took her temperature at 9:30. It had been 97.4, only twenty-five minutes earlier. Somehow in that short time, even though her temperature hadn't descended to anything near a dangerous level, she was showing a symptom that could itself prove fatal: the dreamlike, happy state of hypothermia, which had led directly to countless fatalities when people decided to lie down in a snowpack or wherever they found themselves for a relaxing, blissful nap. She retook her temperature and found it had somehow gone down to 97.1. As she reflected, she realized that the progression of hypothermia could not be captured by data. Data was relevant—important—but it was clear that, even though her temperature had not fallen to a hazardous level, she was entering a more dangerous realm. That was when she had the idea that would save her life: She set the alarm on her phone for two o'clock, programming it with a message to herself: "Get out." It felt a little dramatic, if not ridiculous, but at the same time, it helped her feel more relaxed than she had since coming into the room. She returned the phone to the table, pushed her chair back from it, so the fans could reach her once more, and began to stare again.

Right away, the euphoria began overspreading her heart, her mind, and her body. It was one of the more beautiful feelings she had experienced, and she briefly wondered if anyone had ever been addicted to hypothermia. If people felt what she felt, she was sure some would want to feel it more than once.

Part of what she enjoyed was freedom from the rigidly logical nature of her thoughts. Though no scientist, she had an intensely rational mind. It wasn't surprising that she worked in the high-pressured, cerebral news world. Now, though, for one of the first times in her life, thoughts came out of order, each more beautiful than the last: *The Fifty-Niners are not evil. No one is evil. I love being cold, especially when it makes me feel warm. I love my children. I love Keith. This room is beautiful. I am a good person. I wonder what time it is? I hope I can stay here all day. I must do this again. I should have that mole on my hand removed. I can't believe I've been living indoors for so long. I thought I would get hungry, but I'm not.*

Her phone alarm sounded like a beautiful symphony being carried to her by a gentle breeze across an alpine lake. *I want to listen to this forever,* she thought. After five minutes of it, she started to recognize it as being someone's iPhone. Again, the disconnected thoughts came: *Whoever's phone that is, they should probably turn it off eventually. iPhones are incredible; I love my iPhone. How could I have ever felt stressed by the sound of my iPhone alarm? The sound is so beautiful. I hope the person whose phone it is never turns it off. It's so beautiful.* And then it floated up to her, the one idea that would prove the difference between life and death: *Erica, the phone is yours, and you have to answer it to survive.*

Forcing herself into a state of wakefulness sufficient to turn off the alarm was akin to climbing a mountain. There was a sequence to be followed: remembering the rational message she had received, who she was, what was happening in this room, why it was so hard to remember everything, how to push herself up from a horizontal surface (of the floor she had somehow collapsed upon), how to get to her knees (since standing seemed to be out of the question), and how to crawl. Finally, she crawled to the table, picked up her insistent phone (which still sounded strangely beautiful), and stared at it before turning off the alarm. That was when she saw the message: "Get out." She knew she wasn't in the habit of leaving herself messages such as this; she took it at face value. Still more than a little foggy, she watched herself push the button to turn off the alarm, fight to get the phone in her shorts pocket, pull the fans' electric cords from the table-top sockets, and clumsily stow them in the duffel bag. She was also on the verge of assembling the thermometers to stash them when she realized she wanted to take her temperature before ending the experiment. By force of will, she made sense of using the thermometer, which showed 93 degrees. Her duffel packed and zipped shut, she stepped into the hallway and headed for the elevators, summoning an Uber in the Wi-Fi–enabled car on the way down.

In the back seat of the Uber, she sent texts to her husband ("home in 10") and Ben ("safe and secure, thx again").

As her fog lifted during the trafficky Uber ride uptown, she wondered how unusual it was for giddiness and guilt to compete for a person's attention.

17

Amy's and Whit's senses of selfless concern for the people at risk of freezing to death in their homes were similar. While she trusted that science and industry would develop better forms of energy with time, she knew that Whit was right about wind and solar power: They were inefficient and bore environmental risks that got downplayed in the media.

That didn't mean she was even a little prepared to be the widow of a Fifty-Niner. She mostly took him at his word that he would not leave her and the children behind, but she also felt that making Whit's role public would make him that much less liable to find his way into a 59-degree laboratory with sensors strapped to his body. She preferred to be surgical in outing him. As a first step, she set up an email account that no one could trace to her. Although tempted to send a message identifying him to a media outlet, she feared the consequences—including the chance that he would learn what she had done. Instead, she looked up the Chilean artist who had painted Mike O'Brien and had his portrait brought down on her head. The woman's work was having moderate commercial success, but, more important, it was affecting the debate about the morality of the Fifty-Niners, if not changing minds about global warming itself. Finding the Chilean online was no problem; in addition to a social media presence, she had a website, and the site had a contact page. With Whit in the study working on a paper and the children down for the night, Amy pulled out her laptop in the basement and began to type: "Whit Thorgason knows several Fifty-Niners and probably knew Mike. Good luck. —A friend." Remorse found her instantly. Operating in the shadows wasn't like her.

But now, she would have to live with the results of her secretive action. She reached to pull her laptop closed when she heard the ping of a response. She felt nervous electricity run through her as she opened it:

"Are you Whit's wife? —J.T."

Amy waited as long as she could before typing a reply: "Yes." She paused again and then pushed SEND.

The reply came back in less than a minute: "I prefer to chat." That was fine with her. After agreeing on a chat platform, they began a conversation both would have thought impossible an hour before.

JUANITA: thank you for the kind words about my paintings

AMY: only good thing to come out of this

JUANITA: this is not a tragedy ... Miguel's death wasn't for nothing

AMY: I didn't mean that, not exactly, anyway. I wrote out of desperation, hoping it might help my husband achieve part of what he wants without following in Mike's footsteps. We have children

JUANITA: and you are a scientist, too? what kind?

AMY: chemist ... my team works on alternative fuels, ironically enough

JUANITA: that is a beautiful thing ... Miguel said that within three generations, big things might come from that sort of work

AMY: Hopefully not that long, but I appreciate the vote of confidence, nonetheless

JUANITA: how can I be of service to you? do you really fear he will be a Fifty-Niner?

AMY: I don't know what is possible ... half his friends have become Fifty-Niners, which has taken a toll on him and our family

JUANITA: I would help you if I could

AMY: what if you painted Whit before he becomes a Fifty-Niner ... he would get on the news and maybe say a few things?

JUANITA: but not die

AMY: exactly

JUANITA: send me a few photos of him

AMY: sure

JUANITA: I will need three weeks

AMY: OK ... I am grateful

JUANITA: And I am to you for reaching out to me

AMY: bye for now

JUANITA: bye

When, eighteen days later, the painting was complete, Juanita wrote something different within the bottom third of the canvas than she had on the others: "FIFTY-NINER?" She knew there were news people following her work; a dozen or more requests for interviews had come since the first on the steps of St. James by-the-Sea. She hadn't come close to agreeing to any of them. She knew that whatever the intentions of the journalists approaching her, they were part of a machine that chewed up and spat out anyone who didn't serve it.

But she agreed with Amy that, for Whit, being approached by journalists was his best hope not to become a Fifty-Niner and get his message across, as fraught as it might prove.

Within hours of Juanita posting her painting on Instagram, the word was out throughout the Western media about the guy depicted; he was some glaciologist from the University of Colorado named Whit Thorgason. His parents had been famous climate deniers who had lost their jobs at the University of Washington. The son seemingly felt he had to justify his parents' work. It was bright and early the following day when Erica, aided by Whit's having left his cellphone number on his university curriculum vitae, had sent a text message. It had been three weeks since her experiment in the conference room, but as she pressed SEND, it felt like it had been three hours. She shivered.

It had been a simple message: "I'm a producer for NBC Nightly News . . . can we talk?"

She let ten minutes pass.

Then she sent a second message: "I've done some research into where you guys are coming from . . . let me know if you have time for a call."

Her phone rang fifteen seconds later.

"This is Erica," she answered.

"My name is Whit. What was the research you did?"

"I set up a fifty-nine-degree room with fans and sat in it in shorts, a T-shirt, and flip-flops. I almost died."

"That was stupid."

"I know it was. Santa Claus got to me, though."

"Silvestras was a good person," Whit said.

"I imagine most of you are," Erica said. "His family approving his becoming a Fifty-Niner changed this for me."

"I feel like you're setting me up for something here," Whit said.

"And I'm not," Erica said. "Why did she paint you? And why are you still alive?"

"She probably painted me because I'm *with* the Fifty-Niners, but I can't die," Whit said. "I have kids."

"You must feel unbelievable guilt."

"Yep."

"Would you talk about it on camera?"

"Nope."

"You're kidding me."

"I'm not," Whit said. "Only real Fifty-Niners deserve to be seen on camera. Fair is fair."

"That's it?" Erica said.

"I'd be willing to debate one of your go-to scientists about why it's wrong to make energy so expensive that people die needlessly in their homes in the hundreds of thousands every winter."

"You wouldn't want to use long sentences on the air," Erica said. "Just as a head's-up."

"I get that," Whit said.

"I'm not trying to convince you I'm on your side," she said. "But I'd like you to trust me. Is that possible?"

"You said you almost died. What happened?"

"I set an alarm for myself in case I went hypothermic, which I did. I guess I was farther along in the process than I thought because forcing myself to respond to it was unbelievably hard. I wanted to listen to it, ecstatically, as I fell deeper into unconsciousness."

"Why would you risk that?" Whit said. "You had to know you were putting yourself in danger. Are you a parent?"

"I am," Erica said. "I wanted to feel cold, really cold. I don't know exactly why, other than what I've told you."

"It hurts being cold."

"Yes, it does."

"Until it doesn't," Whit said.

"I'll call you when I have something more," she said.

"I'll be here."

Whit, in his office, hung up and thought for a moment before calling Amy. There were things to talk about, but it wasn't the kind of conversation you rushed into blindly. Without doubt, she had communicated with Mike's artist girlfriend and had probably granted the woman permission to paint his likeness with "FIFTY-NINER?" in the bottom third of the canvas.

That much he'd known within an hour of Juanita posting the image of her painting online after a series of friends and colleagues reached out to him. Those reaching out included his boss at the university, who left a voicemail no one wants to get from a boss: "Call me immediately." His boss, the dean of faculty for the graduate school, could not remove him from a tenured post, but he could set in motion processes that were likely to have that effect.

He was trying to decide between calling Amy first or his boss when a call came from the reporter's number.

"What's up?" Whit said, not feeling very formal for some reason.

"We have the director of climatology at NASA willing to debate you on-air tonight. You'll need to go to our affiliate in Denver, and you'll need to be there within 90 minutes. Can you do that?"

"I could, but I'm not leaning in that direction," Whit said.

"Why not?"

"Well, first, thank you, because I know how rare it is for someone with my views to make it onto TV, let alone to get to speak to a person like Jones." He was referring to NASA's Nigel Jones, the long-bearded, half-native New Zealander who headed the agency's climate-modeling division on the Columbia University campus—the Goddard Institute for Space Studies. Jones had been reluctant to participate in a debate since he had lost one at the University of Auckland in 2003 with an Australian comedian who thought climate change was a hoax. Now though, Jones felt the Fifty-Niners were getting more than their share of attention and fancied himself the man to put one of their representatives in his place. Whit had watched a video of the 25-year-old debate several times, and he couldn't shake the idea that Jones had lost because he knew the comedian was right. Jones had never stopped arguing forcefully, but there was something in his eyes that he wouldn't allow himself to say out loud, or so it seemed to Whit.

"And?" Erica said.

"And the two minutes and thirty seconds you probably have found for our segment is insufficient to undo years of disinformation about people in my camp, even if it were just me talking."

"You know the pace of modern news segments," Erica said.

"We all operate within given constraints," Whit said, "but those, in all honesty, are too tight for me."

"I'll try you back," she said.

"I'll be here," he said.

18

"Mom, kids at school said Dad's gonna be on TV."

"Well, that's true," Amy said. It hadn't taken a genius to figure out this conversation was coming. Their older daughter, Molly, and she were in the kitchen.

"They said Dad's a bad scientist." Molly, thirteen, was academically inclined, at least as much as her two parents were. Whit chose not to saddle her with his views on climate, though she knew the bare bones of what his parents had experienced.

"That part is *not* true," Amy said.

"I know it's not, but they said it," Molly said. "A lot of them said it."

"A lot of people say a lot of things," Amy said.

"That's not all they said."

"What else?"

"They said Dad gets money from the oil companies and that only fools and evil people think climate change isn't real."

"You maybe should talk to your dad about that."

"He's in New York, Mom!"

"He might have time to FaceTime with you."

"I shouldn't distract him," Molly said.

"He can't be distracted."

"I'll call."

There was a reason Whit Thorgason was in New York: Erica

Nagle had come through. It didn't mean anyone in power at NBC thought he was less than crazy and evil, but the Fifty-Niners had been remarkably good for ratings, which the executives called "truth." Incredibly, the network had given the green light to a one-hour, moderated debate between Whit and Nigel Jones for Thursday, May 27th—two days away.

The network was putting him up at The Plaza, and he had flown to JFK, first class. He sensed that he was a lamb that unseen forces were fattening for slaughter. But if it was indeed Jones debating him, it shouldn't be as bad as all that. He should do fine. At times, even so, it was hard to believe that things were playing out this way. He sat on the edge of his bed, staring at a darkened, lifeless TV screen. Could he save the world by what he would say to people through boxes like this? Probably not, but he would try. His phone made the sound it did when one of the kids wanted to video chat. It was Molly. When he pressed ACCEPT, her face flickered onto his iPhone. His daughter was wearing the beat-up crimson hooded sweatshirt she wore whenever she needed comfort and sat on the edge of her bed in her room.

"Hey, love, what's up?" Whit said.

"Kids at school."

"Well, we both knew that was coming, right?"

"Kind of," Molly said. "You've told me a couple of things about why you think what you do. But I don't honestly understand."

"It's not your fight," he said.

"That's what you always said, but it kind of is now."

"I get that," Whit said.

"They've been teaching me about global warming since, like, kindergarten."

"That's the perfect age to teach it to," he said.

"Dad!"

"Sorry."

"And there's no way that so many scientists could all be wrong about something this important," Molly said.

"The first scientists concerned about it weren't wrong," he said.

"Okay," she said.

"But once we learned more about different feedbacks in the system and more precisely what past climate was like, it became clear to anyone with an objective mind that now is a pretty good time to be alive, climatologically."

"Then why are there so many hurricanes and fires and floods and droughts?"

"The short answer is that they get ad clicks."

"That's crazy," she said.

"No, it's not. People are powerfully drawn to disasters, specifically when they see them on their devices and TV screens. It's a kind of addiction."

"So, you're saying a worldwide addiction to disaster, combined with a worldwide conspiracy among scientists and media outlets, has created a situation in which only my dad is right about climate and a bunch of Nobel-prize winners are wrong?"

"It does sound crazy," he said.

"And?"

"And it's not *just* me."

"It's you and some crazy weirdos who kill themselves with hypothermia," she said.

"They're not crazy. Not one of them is crazy."

"Were you ever a kid?" she said. "Do you know what this is like for me?"

"I hate how this is for you. And I probably don't know how it feels."

"You don't."

"I'm here to listen; can you tell me?"

"It would be easier if you were a Nazi."

"That stung. And I'm not sure you're right."

"I was making a point," she said. "And I am right."

"Well, I hope not," Whit said.

"Even if you are right, and I'm not sure you are, this is still a complete nightmare. I had friends, Dad. Past tense."

"Your real friends will stick by you."

"That's just something people say," Molly said.

"No, it's not," he said. "It's true. It may not seem like it for a while, probably longer than either of us would want. But you'll come through this with some friends."

"*Some?*"

"I know you don't want me to lie to you," he said.

"This is one time, Dad, when I wish you would."

"I've got to get ready for the show. Can I call you later?"

She had hung up.

He supposed it was her way of showing him what things felt like. *Fair enough*, he thought.

19

Erica's star had always burned brightly at the network, but it was burning even brighter lately. Since she had almost taken her own life researching cold's effects on the body in the conference room, she was in the zone, big time.

Everyone in the building was aware tonight's debate was her brainchild, and plenty of people who mattered at the other networks knew it, too. Their way of responding to the buzz generated was to report on the debate how they would on a Super Bowl or Olympics they weren't carrying. It was crazy. Her phone never stopped vibrating with texts. She bought a new one just for family. Indeed, she had come close to throwing the old one away, and she thought that she still might by the end of the night.

Ben had shown happiness for her, but there had been a layer of distance between them since the experiment. She had never told him how close she had come to not coming out of the conference room, but he knew her well enough to glean that it was, at a minimum, a weirder experience than she let on. She and Chip were about to walk past each other in the hall when Chip paused his stride.

"If it craters, it's yours," he said.

"And if it pulls in millions for the network, it's yours," she said.

"I always said you were astute."

"Well, it's good to know you're rooting for me," she said.

Ben was waiting at her office door, a sign of the new strain between them. Until recently, he would have walked through the door and waited for her at her desk.

"Come on in," she said as she slipped past.

"Stressed about tonight?"

"Not my style," she said. "You know me."

"I think I do. I don't know what happened in the conference room that day."

"It was great. I learned a lot."

"Fox had a guest who said, 'NBC is coddling deniers.' You must be proud."

"*Truth* is *truth*, for starters, Erica said. "Second, are you surprised a Fox guest would say NBC's the problem?"

"You are giving volcano guy a platform," he said. "You changed in that room."

"I'm not sure I did," she said. "Whatever happened only made me more of who I always was. I still don't know how I feel about the Fifty-Niners, but I know they're not merely bad people."

"Because you let yourself get cold?" Ben said, his gray eyes narrowing.

"Why are you so skeptical of me?"

"I don't think I'm the skeptic here."

"You know what I mean," she said.

"What happened that day?"

"It hurt. Cold hurts. And these guys aren't doing it for attention or because they like suffering. They think they're saving people."

"And?" he said.

"And we all want to save people."

"And?"

"And maybe they're right," she said. "Are you even going to listen to Thorgason tonight?"

"Not if I can help it," he said.

"Maybe they're right specifically that we in the media have been profiting off this a long time," she said. "Maybe we've been blind to our own motives. Did you think that's impossible?"

"I think you *still* have hypothermia."

"Who says I ever had hypothermia?"

"I may not know exactly what happened on the eighteenth floor, but I know that much," he said. "I'm not stupid, and I know you."

"Just keep an open mind when it's on. I've got to meet with Chip. Are you looped in on that?"

"I'm helping PR with a press release."

"Bullshit," she said.

"No lie," he said.

"This is a strange moment in time."

"Ya think?" Ben said.

"Open mind," she said.

"Always," he said. When he stepped out of Erica's office, he felt more comfortable outside it than he had in it. It was a first.

CHIP HAD entertained talk of a live studio audience for the debate but decided to proceed without one. An individual on one of the upper floors expressed concern that if Thorgason started to perform well, he could turn the audience in his favor. No one was willing to take that risk—neither in terms of the effect on the broader debate around the country nor when it came to how it would make the network look. So, production assistants set up the studio with chairs and tables and nothing else; behind the moderator's table would be seated a rising young star from

MSNBC. The choice solved a lot of problems. First, the network going with someone from its left wing appeased environmental extremists, who were up in arms over the mere existence of the debate. Second, the choice communicated that this wasn't an NBC News event properly, even if it was in name. Without a *Nightly News* anchor or, at the least, a gray-haired, long-tenure reporter as moderator, the debate had less gravitas than it might have had. When it came down to it, if anything terrible happened, the whole thing could be hung around the neck of Erica Nagle, at least internally, whose idea it had been.

The event was scheduled to follow *The Nightly News*, which ended at 7 P.M., eclipsing the network affiliates' 7 o'clock local news broadcasts. Three stations protested by refusing to go with the network feed. One was the Denver affiliate, KUSA, which served not only Greater Denver but also Boulder, one of the Climatists' regional meccas. After a series of angry phone calls from department heads and two university presidents, the station ownership team reasoned that whatever friction the move cost them with New York was worth it in terms of avoiding boycotts—or worse. Beyond the San Francisco Bay Area affiliate, KNTV, broadcasting out of San Jose, there was one other station not to go with the feed. The station was KCWY out of Casper, Wyoming, where climate-change belief was far from strong, and most considered their local news more reliable than national news.

Word was circulating in the studio designated for the debate that *truth* would be unparalleled for a one-off news event on a random weeknight. In addition to generating high dollar amounts spent on advertising slots, an event like this created ratings bumps for the shows that followed, sometimes for the rest of the night, less often for the rest of the week. And, in this

case, everyone involved could detect the collective interest from
the country even as they neared the studio, partly from seeing
fellow staffers' frightened but interested eyes, partly from the
unusual quiet. A few groups of people were in the hall, more than
average, and they mostly communicated with hand gestures,
nods, glances, and the odd whispered word. Erica was reaching
for the studio door handle to go in when she heard someone say
her name behind her in a full-throated speaking voice. The fact
that it was Rita Guzman's didn't help. Under the circumstances,
it was enough to make her jump out of her skin.

Erica turned around to face her rival; Guzman was all the
producers' nemesis, and she didn't lose. She was wearing a white
blouse under a gray power suit that showed off the body she
maintained somehow, despite the long hours she was known to
put in. Her shoulder-length brown hair, with a few white strands
to convey seriousness, was held back by an expensive-looking
tortoiseshell hair clip. Her brown eyes, constantly assessing, always full of ambition but also laced with sorrow, looked Erica
up and down.

"You've got a lot riding on this," Guzman said.

"No kidding," Erica said.

"They flipped you," Guzman said.

"Who flipped me?" Erica said. "And what did they flip me
from and to?"

"Don't be coy."

"I didn't get *flipped*," Erica said.

"You're giving them the biggest stage they could ever get to
spout lies," Guzman said. "Well done."

"Do you honestly believe they kill themselves because they're
trying to destroy the earth?" Erica said.

"Yes," Guzman said.

"Well, you're right," Erica said. "I don't believe that, and I guess it means maybe I did get flipped. I don't think they're going to win, and I don't think it's going to go well for me here after tonight, but let's see what happens, okay?"

"It's sad," Guzman said. "You were my favorite rival."

"And?"

"And I thought you'd be there for me to fight a lot longer," Guzman said.

"You're sad, Rita."

"Sad and employed."

"I've got to go in," Erica said. "I have things to do."

"Do you need help with anything?" Guzman asked without evident sarcasm.

"I do, but it would be hard to trust you right now. I'm sorry," Erica said.

"Let me know if you change your mind," Guzman said.

"I'll do that," Erica said. With that, she turned, opened the studio door, and disappeared.

20

Gertie Robinson woke up thinking of tea. She had been chilly so long that the cold had become part of her, like a painful extra limb. Scalding tea was one of the principal means she had of trying to shake off the chill, but it was working less well of late. A decade before, sipping two or three teas during the day made a difference. But back then, she could afford to set the thermostat at 66.

On New Year's Day of 2020, with her bills mounting, she lowered it to 64. She had felt uncomfortably cold through February. Still, she learned that she could stay almost comfortable by sitting in front of the television in gloves, a hat, and layers of wool clothing, with a blanket on top.

By 2024, her most recent effort to economize had proved futile, with her monthly electricity charge rising from 200 pounds a month in winter to more than 240, which meant she was paying more to be colder than she was before. She barely bought fresh bread anymore; she hadn't had a new pair of shoes in a decade and a half. Going out for tea with her dearest friend, Nan, went from a weekly treat to a monthly one, to one rarer than that. Café prices had become painfully high.

Lowering the thermostat to 62 on New Year's Day 2025, Gertie had known she was in for more suffering; she hadn't been wrong.

She had spent only a few days outside the shire during her life. For starters, she knew no one outside it, and if there had been anyone to visit, there had been little enough money for travel. Grimsby, where she had spent her life, wasn't a world capital, but it was her world. A cousin who had made it to Paris had sent a postcard in 1981; it hung on the wall of her galley kitchen. The card was a photograph of the booksellers and their stalls across from Nôtre-Dame; it showed lush tree foliage and passersby in shirtsleeves, a happy summer scene. She could almost feel the breeze as it ruffled the hair of one of the people on the card. She stared at it sometimes, though she had already memorized its every detail. "Ah, Gertie," she would say. "You won't be strolling the banks of the Seine today." But she did exactly that in her heart, as many days as not.

Her son, Jason, had been a fishing captain, as rugged as his father and as successful. When the new apartment towers went up, he insisted that she accept the apartment as a gift, even though she could support herself at the time. They each liked that she could see him through her picture window as his boat came and went. During the years since losing him, she had taken comfort in the view of the glittering sea, one she reckoned as beautiful as any. It was *his* glittering sea, no less after he died in a storm like those that had claimed men for as long as boats had come and gone from Grimsby.

Of late, the fishing industry had shrunk to a tenth of its former size. The families who had sent sons, husbands, and fathers onto the North Sea to bring back cod now sent them to harvest electricity by servicing the 200-odd turbines towering above the waters offshore. Nan's boy, Roderick, was one of the former fishermen responsible for slowing the degradation of the massive turbines in the face of sun, rain, snow, and wind from above and saltwater from below. The turbines could be pretty to look at, but Gertie was aware of what they'd done to her electric bill, of the suffering they'd caused her.

On this dark Friday, there was nothing to see through the window but fog. For three days, a cold drizzle had held sway over the estuary and surrounding waters. She'd noticed upon arising that her thinking was none too clear, which she first thought to attribute to flu or a cold. But as she put on the kettle, she realized she had no symptoms.

She stood near the stove as the water heated to draw a tiny amount of heat from it. As she waited, she found herself replaying dreams about being cold she had been having. Gertie had come to fear having them the way children fear the recurrence of nightmares. As a girl, she'd dreamed of intruders, kidnappers, and bogeymen of a hundred sorts, but there had been one happy part to the experience—relief upon awakening that it had only been a nightmare. There was no delight in dreaming about feeling cold and then waking up feeling the same way.

The year before, Gertie had dreamed of walking the hills outside Grimsby in her nightgown as giant white snowflakes floated down from a nighttime sky. She'd woken with a start, shivering. Ever since she had slept beneath all the blankets she owned.

The kettle whistled, and she poured boiling water over a Red Rose tea bag in her favorite cup. A gift from Jason, it was cream colored with red lettering spelling "BEST MA AROUND." Gertie dreaded ever breaking it, but not enough to stop using it. As the tea finished brewing, she drifted to the thermostat. This year on New Year's Day, she had again turned it down—to 61. Doing so made it possible to continue covering medication, co-op fees on the apartment, food (little of it worth eating), a few necessities, and an electric bill that had tripled in thirty years, despite her diminished current use. Standing before the thermostat in her slippers and heavy layers of pajamas and robes, she thought for a long moment about turning it up to something extravagant like 65, just for the day. She glared at the tiny piece of technology as if it were an adversary with whom she could engage in a stare-down. Then, resigned to her fate, she returned to the kitchen, lifted the mug to her lips, and poured the piping-hot tea down in quick, painful swallows. To her disappointment, it left her no warmer.

She moved to the window, drawing the curtains and standing with her face inches from the glass. She could just make out a shadow twenty stories below her where the Dock Tower stood and beneath it the fog-shrouded lights along the waterfront.

There were thousands and thousands of mornings like this one stretching into her past. Cold mist and the zero visibility that came with it were nearly as common here as the daybreak itself. Still, Gertie felt a strange pull to witness the glimmering light of the sun dappling the water, and Jason's private presence within it, one more time. She stood in front of the large window for three minutes, asking God to do this. When nothing happened, she couldn't think of anything to do but turn, take her station in her upholstered chair, pick up the TV remote, and push the power button. "Not to be," she said.

It was 6:02 A.M.

The BBC morning news program was just ramping up, with some impossibly young meteorologist doing her best to give hope to a country that had seen miserable weather for the better part of six weeks. Gertie kept the volume low enough that she was less likely to initiate entire conversations with the stupid thing, something she'd witnessed herself do more than she would want to admit. By keeping it just loud enough to discern

what those on the air were saying, it kept her attention without
tempting her to speak, except when it lulled her to sleep, which
had been happening more. She could scarcely follow the meteorologist. "High pressure" were the only words the woman spoke
that Gertie processed, out of hundreds said. And, without
knowing she was doing it, Gertie repeated "high pressure" in a
soft hush. A sense that all was well with the world flooded
through her. She had alternately loved and hated the Beeb for
decades, but now the casually beautiful, forty-something pre-
senters appeared to her like treasured friends who had popped
over for a cuppa and were glad to be in her presence. She was
glad to be in their presence, too. Indeed, she was the happiest
she had been in her life, including the morning Jason had come
into the world and the day she had married his dad. This moment, shimmering and comforting at once, contained those days
and the dozen other truly happy ones of her life. They were all
happening at once within her now, and she knew that she would
never be cold again. Cold was for all the days before this one; it
was for other people. It was her ancient enemy, and it had finally
conceded.

As true happiness, beyond euphoria, began to settle in, the
door opened, and she turned and saw the face of someone she
hadn't counted on seeing again. It was Jason. He was in the same
gear he'd been wearing the day he'd been lost at sea. His hair
and face and everything he was wearing were dripping, as
though he had just been plucked from the water. His eyes met
hers and communicated in a flash that she was wrong to fear his
death, and wrong to fear death at all. She stood, easily, as though
her body weighed nothing, and their embrace, so long delayed,
was filled with radiant light.

III

Kick over the wall, 'cause government's to fall
How can you refuse it?
Let fury have the hour, anger can be power
Do you know that you can use it?

—The Clash, "Clampdown"
(Songwriters: Joe Strummer and Mick Jones)

21

The NBC News green room Whit found himself in was, he absently thought, slightly larger than the master bedroom he and Amy shared. It had an off-white, U-shaped leather couch, a mini fridge, a mirrored wall, and smaller mirrors on two of the three other walls. There was a wall-mounted wood clothing rack, recently vacuumed gray carpeting, a coffee table strewn with magazines and the day's newspapers (and now his dinner), and an intercom next to the door.

He felt like a boxer before a match; his opponent was presumably in a room much like this one, possibly on the same floor. He had ordered roast chicken with quinoa and vegetables, a pepperoni pizza, and a Caesar salad. It wasn't necessarily his "last meal," per se, but anyone who saw the quantity of food on the coffee table and the large, athletic, and solitary man eating it couldn't mistake the similarity between this silent dinner and actual last meals of the condemned. He was eating the food with intense focus, for one thing. For another, he was eating the feast alone and felt about as alone as he ever had. Even if he were to perform well in the debate, the consequences would be many, some of them predictable, others not; it gave him pause and deepened his sense of isolation. Working at a university again would be unlikely. The prospect of being banished from his intellectual home was like a brick in his stomach. There was also curiosity to see how things would be on the other side. For an inmate facing death, the other side meant an afterlife (or not). For Whit, the uncertainty of his own "afterlife" was almost as terrifying. Would he and Amy have any more friends? Would his kids lose *all* theirs, as his daughter feared, and eventually disown him themselves? He had grown up the kind of person who didn't particularly care about what strangers thought of him, but the prospect of being hated by a broad swath of people, including some he loved, was daunting.

For some reason, he thought about his cousin Irwin, who was, presumably, on the Upper West Side, just a few miles away from Rockefeller Center. Chances were good that Irwin, with whom he'd been close when they were teenagers, would have heard about the debate and was sad not to have been called.

A production assistant knocked on the green room door and entered. "I'll be taking you down in twenty minutes," she said. When setting him up in the room earlier, she had told him that her name was Betsy. She kept her brown hair held back in a bun and hid her brown eyes behind tortoiseshell glasses; she wore expensive informal clothing and was pretty in a nerdy, bland way.

"Thank you," Whit said.

"Everything good?" she said.

"Awesome," he said, giving a thumb's-up and then wondering if it looked like the overcompensating gesture of a man about to "die." He was confident, but he wasn't crazy and knew the odds he faced. After eating, he wiped his mouth with a large linen napkin and stood. He went to the clothing rack where he'd left his suit coat hanging and—for the third time since entering the building—reassured himself by patting the left front breast pocket to feel the contents of the inner pocket, which held a prop he intended to use on camera. He could feel the thing's reassuring shape beneath the fabric; it hadn't vanished. He used the private bathroom, quickly hit his knees in prayer, and sat on the couch again. In a moment, the same knock came, followed by the reappearance of Betsy, the assistant.

"Ready for makeup?" she said.

"Um, yes?" Whit said.

As instructed, he followed her to makeup. As he sat in the chair, most of his sun blemishes got hidden, and his wrinkles got smoothed out. The artist altered the hue of his skin to one of the colors the network favored for the newest generation of its ultra-high-definition broadcasts. The tone applied to his skin, one made by a Swiss company, was a trademarked product named Surfer, which would have made him laugh had he known. To his eye, the effect of everything done to his face was over the top, but presumably, it worked on television.

The female makeup artist—in blue jeans, a white blouse, and high heels—reminded him of Cher. She was from Queens and had two kids and a granddaughter on the way, she told him; while working her artistry, she also told him to give the other scientist hell. He hadn't expected that. It seemed some people in the outer boroughs of New York knew the Climatists weren't necessarily the good guys. It was reassuring. "Thank you," he said to the stylist, Tamara.

"Thank *you*," she said, then snapped her gum.

Both the green room and the makeup room had been over-air conditioned; the studio to which Betsy led him was chillier still. He knew it had something to do with the lights tending to overheat and the human beings under the lights getting awkwardly sweaty. The appearance would be his first on TV, and it happened to be a live, national broadcast debating the fate of humanity, more or less. It reminded him of paddling out on the

North Shore during the biggest swells he had surfed. He was focused and upbeat, but there was no denying the unmistakable minor shivering adrenalin in his blood produced. As his eyes adjusted to the darkened surroundings behind the cameras, he saw Betsy, the production assistant, in conversation with a more powerful-looking woman, perhaps a decade and a half older than herself. Before he could start trying to eavesdrop or get a sense of the character of their conversation, the older woman gave him a friendly glance and walked toward him, hand extended for what proved to be a firm handshake.

"Most people are too nervous to eat, or at least to eat much," Erica Nagle said. She had on heels and was wearing a tailored black suit over a white blouse, her medium-length brown hair with gray highlights held back in a studious ponytail.

"I'm not un-nervous," Whit said.

"Of course, you're not," Erica said.

"Can I see the setup?" he asked.

"Sure," she said. She cocked her head to tell him to follow and led him between a pair of cameras that probably cost more than his house. Bathed in near-blinding light was a stage with a semi-circular table, behind which sat chairs for himself and Jones. A smaller, semi-circular table was inset into the larger one, with a chair behind it for the moderator. Cameras were in every direction, poised to capture utterances and facial expressions from the most telling angle at every moment. The proliferation of lenses was intimidating, even before contemplating the millions of eyes to which the cameras would deliver the images captured.

"Which seat will be mine?" Whit asked Erica.

"That will be determined by a coin toss a few minutes before we go on," she said.

"Seriously?" he said.

"I'm afraid so. Do you have a preference?"

"No, I just need to check the vertical clearance above each chair," he said.

"Because?" Erica said.

"I need about eighteen feet," he said.

"Straight overhead?"

"Yes," Whit said, "and the cameras would need to be able to pick up something I'll be holding up there."

"This sounds bad," Erica said.

"It's just a prop," Whit said.

"Which you have on you?" she said.

"Yes," he said, patting the item through his suit coat.

"I'm guessing it's not a helium balloon," she said.

"And you are correct," Whit said.

They stood behind each chair and craned their necks upward. While overhead lights fringed the stage, the space directly above the debate table was unused. To Whit, it looked like the shadowy ceiling was a good twenty-five feet up.

"I'm all set," he said.

"And you can't tell me what the prop is?" she said.

"It's not going to make anything difficult for you, and I think you'll see why it had to be a secret," he said.

"The techs are looking this way, and Jones is in the room," Erica said. Whit just managed not to swivel his head in search of the NASA scientist. Using peripheral vision he had developed in surf lineups, he took in everything within 180 degrees of him as he continued facing Erica. He could see Jones in the shadows, having entered using a door Whit hadn't noticed until now.

"I'll let them mic you up," Erica said.

"I'm still amazed you made this happen," Whit said.

"Good luck," she said, stepping from the platform and exiting between the two cameras they had passed a few minutes before.

"Mr. Thorgason?" said a voice coming from near his right shoulder.

It was the sound technician, a forty-something man with glasses, a red fleece vest—in deference to the studio's frosty temperature—over a white button-up shirt and khaki chinos. He sported ill-considered mutton-chop sideburns making the sparse brown hair atop his head seem sparser still.

"That's me," Whit said.

"I'm Nate," the tech said. "I'm going to be wiring you for sound, okay?" To his credit, he hesitated before approaching Whit and awaited a response.

"Sure, thank you," Whit said.

"I think you guys are crazy," Nate said, "but I respect your commitment."

"Thank you very much," Whit said. "I thought my parents were crazy for their views on this stuff when I was young."

"What if you were right?" Nate said.

"I've considered it," Whit said. "All set?"

"All set," Nate said. "Good luck."

"That's kind," Whit said. Nate retreated into the darkness between cameras as a woman radiating personal power approached Whit from the shadows on his other side. The comings and goings were ethereal if you weren't used to them; he had the sense more than once that he wasn't here at all but instead experiencing a strange dream.

"Dr. Thorgason," the woman said, extending her hand.

"That's me," he said. Like Erica, the woman had an impressive handshake.

"My name is Jessica Cahill," she said. "I'm the director." She was noticeably young, barely 30. On the petite side, she wore a black cashmere cardigan over a black dress with white polka dots and black army boots with two-inch-thick soles.

"Thank you for having me," Whit said.

"I would have never approved it," Cahill said. "Once you and Dr. Jones are seated, I will provide you with the rules of the debate out loud, even though I know you have read them. When we are on the air, Frederick Diaz, the moderator, will provide the rules one last time, mostly for the benefit of everyone at home. There will be a couple of two-minute commercial breaks at nineteen and thirty-nine minutes into the broadcast. Are you glad you came?"

"Not yet," Whit said, "but I'm keeping an open mind." She gave him a look part quizzical, part condescending, then turned and walked to a spot ten feet away—where another tech was wiring Jones for sound—to have, presumably, the same pregame conversation with him, if a warmer version of it.

Whit had only met Jones once. The New Zealander had studied Whit up close while attending a volcanology conference in Reykjavik Whit co-led in 2024, the same year Katla started rumbling. Jones recognized that volcanoes represented a wrinkle in the narrative he and the rest of the Climatists had put before the public. Beyond that, he was canny enough to know which volcanologists, Whit and his closest colleagues chief among them, were likely to be the most problematic. Although Whit didn't say anything in Jones's presence that established beyond doubt his true beliefs, it wasn't hard to understand that a man whose parents had been put out to pasture in the prime of their careers might feel a need to take up their cause.

Whit had looked up several times during the conference to find Jones looking at him coldly. It was slightly alarming but also faintly funny. And when he gave some thought to the stares and the fact that Jones was at the conference in the first place, it was clear that Jones's confidence in the scientific and moral righteousness of his cause must not be total. When someone introduced them a few hours before the end of the conference, Whit couldn't keep himself from shaking the pompous, unathletic man's hand a little more firmly than necessary.

"I didn't have you pegged as a closet volcanologist," Whit said to Jones as the two exchanged pleasantries. "But then, when you're a physicist, I guess everything is your subject if you want it to be."

"I do very little in the closet," Jones said. "And as you're aware, our computer models need the best data on everything in the climate system, even things as exaggerated in their importance as volcanoes."

"Your being here makes me think their importance is greater than you say," Whit said.

"That would be a misinterpretation," Jones said. "It was an absolute pleasure meeting you." With that, he turned, picked out his fellow scientists from Goddard in a little knot a short way away, and hurried to them. That had been that.

Erica Nagle emerged from between a pair of cameras, trailed by Frederick Diaz. A few production assistants appeared out of nowhere, leaving a glass of water at each of the debaters' positions, sweeping non-existent dust from the table with their sleeves, and checking in with the sound techs to ensure everything was a go.

Diaz was dark-haired and dark-eyed, athletic, and with a theatrical but hawk-like presence—just the sort of man people liked to watch read the day's news from the comfort of their homes.

"Gentlemen," he said as he approached the table beside which

Jones and Whit stood. "We will determine who speaks first with a coin toss." He produced a quarter from his suit pants pocket. "Mr. Jones, would you like to call it?"

"Heads," Jones said. One-half Maorian (native New Zealander), Jones wore a long thick beard in which blond and brown streaks vied for prominence; he wore a light-green suit and looked less unassuming than Whit remembered him as being. Diaz flipped the coin a couple of feet into the air, caught it with his palm, turned it onto the back of his other hand, and revealed that it had landed heads. "Mr. Jones, you have the right to speak first or to defer; which do you prefer?"

"I defer," Jones said to no one's great surprise, all the less so to Whit's.

Production assistants ushered Whit and Jones to their seats, showed them the glasses of water in case they were too nervous to notice that they were there, and then, in an instant, vanished from the lighted set. Diaz had taken his seat as well, and Jessica Cahill, the director, stood next to him and delivered the ground rules to calm the participants as much as anything else.

"Opening statements are ninety seconds," she said. "That's going to go by faster than you can believe. Dr. Jones, you won the toss, and you will go second. After opening statements, Mr. Diaz will ask each of you questions. He will name which of you he wishes to answer the question first, and the other of you will have time to comment. Each answer, and each comment on an answer, is limited to seventy-five seconds. Ten minutes before the end of the broadcast, Mr. Diaz will invite you to give closing statements, which are limited to one hundred eighty seconds— three minutes. You will not help your cause by making Mr. Diaz's job as moderator difficult. Honor the time rules and good luck to you both."

22

I'm a surfer and a husband and a dad who loves nature and the world," Whit said. He looked at Diaz, sitting at an angle across from him, as he spoke, but he could also see Jones out of the corner of his eye. Jones was all but wincing at every word he uttered as though the words constituted physical blows. "My opponent, Dr. Jones, is a brilliant man trying to do his part to save the world. But his good heart, mind, and intentions have been distorted by noble cause corruption. It's a process that got underway in the climate science community before he even received his doctorate, in physics, by the way. But he has taken noble cause corruption to new heights by joining a team that changed the historical temperature record of Reykjavik, Iceland, among other places, so that instead of showing steady temperatures for the past eighty years, Reykjavik now shows strong warming. Please, Dr. Jones, in your introductory remarks, explain why NASA changed Reykjavik's data, manually lowering the temperatures recorded during the 1930s so that the narrative of climate change would look more compelling than it is. How is *that* science? And will you promise never to change the historical temperature record of any other location in the future?" As Whit said the last word, a red light came on in the center of the table. He had used the exact time allotted.

On the surface, which was all the cameras could capture, Diaz looked as composed as ever. But there was something in his eyes, Whit saw, that revealed surprise, maybe dismay. "Dr. Jones?" Diaz said.

"There were reasons why NASA adjusted Reykjavik's temperature record, mathematical reasons. For the record, that adjustment happened under my predecessor at Goddard, Gabriel Simpson, who was taken from this earth far too early in 2024. But that is not why we are here this evening," Jones said. "I am here tonight because the planet upon which we live and depend for our survival is undergoing dangerous changes, including unprecedented temperature increases; worsening storms, droughts, forest fires, and floods; mass extinctions; and on and on. There is no disputing any of this. Nor has there been any disputing any of this, realistically, for at least a few decades. Fortunately, the overwhelming majority of scientists recognize the reality of the crisis we are facing and are trying to do something about it by sounding warnings while there is yet time. I have no idea whether Dr. Thorgason is a good, bad, or any other kind of man. It does not matter what kind of man he is. What matters is that these colleagues of his taking their own lives in this bizarre and unscientific show has introduced doubt in the minds of certain members of the public. It is time tonight for these tragic and purposeless suicides to cease. Dr. Thorgason no doubt imagines he is restoring the good name of his parents, who were also climate deniers, by being the face of the Fifty-Niners' desperate conspiracy. Ironically, he is merely heaping further shame on himself and them." The red light in the center of the table had come on after the word "deniers," but Diaz allowed Jones to finish.

"Dr. Thorgason, the first question is for you," Diaz said. "You indicate that you love nature, but what kind of nature-lover would defend choices that have left the globe scorched and its inhabitants in peril?"

"I do love nature," Whit said, "and I am glad you asked. There are a lot of ways to measure heat in the ocean-atmosphere system. Temperature is not necessarily the best way, and that's not only because people like Dr. Jones and Dr. Simpson, may he rest in peace, can change the temperature record as they see fit. Another way, and to my mind a better way, is to look at sea level, which we're told all the time is on the verge of drowning half the planet's population. The problem is that sea level is never stable and can't be stable. And the last time we were in a pause in the Ice Age, as we are now and have been for eleven thousand years, sea level was a good amount higher than it is today. That was because of greater amounts of heat in the system over a substantial period, enough to accomplish some serious melting. And that is why—" with this, Whit fished from his breast pocket out what looked like a standard tape measure, but which cost $130 and could be extended twenty feet without bending— "I have this item. I want to show people where sea level was the last time the Ice Age took a break, a hundred and fifteen thousand years ago." Whit extended the end of the tape measure at an angle so that it just missed the shoulder of Diaz, whose shocked eyes were now visible to all, on set and at home. Whit stopped when the end of the tape jutted out 15 feet, about five feet over Diaz's shoulder. Whit had taped a piece of paper to the end, and as he pivoted the base of the tape measure so that the end of the tape rotated to a spot over his head, two different camera operators zoomed in on something printed on the paper. In careful block lettering were the words "SEA LEVEL LAST TIME." Before completing his answer, Whit slowly craned his neck and looked at the top of the tape measure, taking it in himself.

While the message would have been in shadows near the ceiling, a fast-thinking lighting technician had directed a floor-based spotlight for it to be viewable. "For anyone wondering how high the end of that tape measure is, it's fifteen feet. Sea level last time the Ice Age took a break was fifteen feet higher than today. I don't know about anyone else, but that gives me pause when I hear the words 'unprecedented warming.'"

He looked toward Diaz again, who dropped his eyes from his glance, searched his prep notes for a moment, and then looked in Jones's direction before asking him to respond.

"Dr. Jones, your response?"

"We can argue about the meaning of the word 'unprecedented,' but it's not in anyone's interest for us to do so," Jones said, maintaining eye contact with Diaz in such a way as to make it seem he didn't know Whit was there beside him at the table. "There are myriad destructive periods in Earth's history that no sane person would wish to experience in their lifetime. That doesn't mean we have to put our heads in the sand while the climate we have become accustomed to enters a new dangerous phase owing to human activity. Dr. Thorgason and his small group of suicidal deniers are entitled to their own opinions about whether it's acceptable for sea level to return to past levels when that would effectively mean drowning most of the world's great cities. However, fortunately, the overwhelming majority of climatologists have proven beyond any reasonable doubt that we are in the last years of hope for ourselves, our children, and our children's children. And Dr. Thorgason's tape-measure cannot change that simple fact."

"Thank you, Dr. Jones," Diaz said. His shoulders and face had relaxed during Jones's response. This was a scientist saying the same thing that all great scientists had said throughout his journalism career; right was not wrong; up was not down; the sky was not purple with green pinstripes across it; climate cycles were not just part of life on Earth. He was profoundly relieved. "Dr. Jones, the second question is for you. You made several public statements to the effect that you would 'never' engage in a public debate again after you lost to a comedian in a debate about climate change in New Zealand a couple of decades ago, yet here you are. Why?"

"I meant it when I said that, as anyone who knows me can attest," Jones said. "Listen, not only have scientists formed a consensus that humankind's activities have put us on a collision course with climate catastrophe, but just about all well-informed non-scientists have reached the same conclusion. And we're beginning to wean ourselves from the source of the problem— fossil fuels—in a serious, sustained, and meaningful way. And then suddenly, you have these desperate and angry so-called scientists stirring up doubt among the public again. That's bad enough. But what changed my mind, truthfully, was my mother telling me that the Fifty-Niners had raised doubts within her. My mum is intellectually fierce and well-informed and has studied this subject more than most with me as her son, and yet she said she had never really looked at climate cycles until she watched one of the Fifty-Niners' videos. She asked: Was I sure about all of this? And she also mentioned a friend of hers had a brother who died after leaving his thermostat too low. To make a long story short, I am here to stop good people like my mother from wondering if the deniers could be right. Believe me: The deniers are not the good guys in this. No more than the Holocaust deniers are."

"Thank you, Dr. Jones," Diaz said with evident satisfaction. "Dr. Thorgason, your response?"

"I am grateful to Dr. Jones for drawing this link between those of us with a different view from him in the climate science community and Holocaust deniers. Those on my side have been dealing with this for thirty years; the comparison is surely the ugliest piece of propaganda I have witnessed. First, the Nazis were real, and they slaughtered six million Jewish men, women, and children using various horrifying means, including gas chambers. I have made it my business to make certain that my children know the ins and outs of the Holocaust, because it is one of the most important and difficult pieces of human history and, therefore, part of my responsibility as a parent. I have read many books and articles about the Holocaust; I have many Jewish friends; and I have wept my share of tears over the tragic deeds perpetrated by the Nazis. But people at home should ask themselves, 'If Dr. Jones's side has the superior science backing them up, why don't they just share that science? Why do they smear people of goodwill who happen to disagree with them in this way?' The answer is that they do not have superior science, but they are surprisingly skilled at public relations, even and especially when it comes to actual propaganda. The most important part of Dr. Jones's answer to your question, though, was not the smear. That had to do with his family friend perishing from leaving the thermostat too low to sustain human life in his home. Before going on, I would like to ask for a moment of silence for this unnamed man who died of cold in his home."

Whit closed his eyes, bowing his head ever so slightly as he did so. Diaz had returned to his startled-deer-in-the-headlights look, bouncing his gaze from Whit to Jones and back again. Jones, crucially, made the first of several miscalculations by failing to understand that when he rolled his eyes, as he did in response to Whit's request for a moment of silence, it would be seen across the country and around the world. Jones did it the way a thirteen-year-old might in response to a parent's assertion of authority. He opened his mouth in a sarcastic yawn for emphasis, forgetting that though Thorgason was the only one speaking, that did not mean that the camera operators would be blind to the look on his face. Indeed, two of them saw the early movements in his features as his face began the gesture; they both zoomed in. Viewers at home saw it as clear as day. Jones did not care about the man who had died; at most, he considered his death an irritating distraction, hardly worth a moment of silence. It wasn't a good look for a man on TV, but it was not entirely his fault. As someone who had spent his professional life sounding the alarm about excess heat in the atmosphere, people dying of cold in their homes still seemed like an abstraction to him, like a thing not wholly real. At least it did so to the public part of him.

Jones glanced at one of the camera operators who had zoomed in on him, realizing after it was too late that he'd become what the camera operators found important. One of their cameras had its red light on, and Jones knew it meant something awful had just happened. He struggled to put on the expression of a man who found the needless deaths of human beings from cold temperatures in their home worthy of compassion. But doing so eluded him. In desperation, he strove for a look of simple neutrality. However, what everyone saw instead was the face of an indignant child caught in a lie.

"May I say something?" Jones said.

"I'm sorry, Dr. Jones," Diaz said, "the next question is for Dr. Thorgason."

"I would just like to correct a misimpression," Jones said.

"I'm sorry, Dr. Jones," Diaz said, looking somewhat pained.

"You will have your chance. Dr. Thorgason, in the past ten years alone, there have been nearly two hundred Category Four or Category Five hurricanes around the globe. The ongoing drought in Central Africa is thought to have caused the deaths of between thirty and fifty thousand children from starvation and malnutrition. Last year's floods in India killed more than ten thousand people. Wildfires in 2026 claimed an estimated forty-five million acres around the globe. After yet another two-year drought, California is in its most stringent water rationing in history. I could go on, but we have limited time. Are you and the Fifty-Niners honestly willing to look the American public and the rest of the world in the eye and tell them that this is normal and that you're okay with it? When you're teaching your children about the Holocaust, do you tell them that this modern, human-caused calamity is fine by you?"

"I hear what you're saying," Whit said.

"It's not what *I'm* saying—it's the whole world!" Diaz said before realizing he was interrupting Thorgason. "Please, continue."

"Well, let's say I hear where the whole world is coming from," Whit said. "There has long been a duality about our planet's weather and climate, a light side and a dark side. From bumper crops and benign conditions to famine, destructive droughts, floods, and the rest, not one of us has human ancestors who lived without these two sides of weather and climate. Those who investigate the statistics with a truly open mind learn that now is not a terrible moment to be alive. It's a wonderful time to be alive. Poverty, disease, and premature death are on the run compared to any other time in history; the percentage of people dying from natural disasters has been plummeting for the last century. Now is not a Biblically foretold Apocalypse. Now is a great beginning of an even better period in human history. But people are wrong to look at the images on their screens and imagine that these weather disasters will end if they do what other people tell them to do. They will not end. They cannot end. They are merely a component of life on Earth, sometimes a challenging and overwhelming component. That's the truth, coming from the mouth of a scientist. Freezing people to death in their homes in the name of transitioning away from fossil fuels will not appease the gods, and it will not make the wind stop blowing during hurricane season, no matter what this man, or any other Climatist, tells you. But it will leave behind a new mass killing, a mass killing of cold, one no less real than the mass killings of history, with victims numbering in the tens of millions before all is said and done. I will ask my colleague, 'Which side of this silent, frozen Holocaust do you wish to stand on, with your eyes rolling all the while? How many people freezing to death at home will be enough to get you to reconsider the policies you have forced upon an unsuspecting public?'"

Jones was smart enough not to roll his eyes again, but the urge to do so was there. He had known from two minutes into the proceedings that coming here was the biggest mistake in his career and most likely in his life. The task facing him was to climb down from his exposed position and confer with the other members of the Climatists' upper hierarchy regarding how to undo the damage—somewhere far away from here. But before he could do that, there were the second two-thirds of this debate to be gotten through.

"I'm not blind to the realities of cold weather," he began, surprised, as he did, to see the hard look in Thorgason's eyes soften and Diaz listening with a new level of attentiveness. "My mum has needed help paying her heating bill, which I provide, for more than half my career. And, yes, I see the irony in a man considered by some to be a global warming warrior having to pay to keep his mother alive in wintertime. But the continued existence of winter, and of some winter deaths in a relatively small number of homes, does not begin to disprove the climate crisis, which has been upon us for more than a generation."

"Last year, forty-three thousand people died in the U.K. alone from cold-weather mortality," Whit interrupted. "My team estimates that another five to seven hundred thousand died around the rest of the world, including tens of thousands in the Southern Hemisphere. How dare you call that a small number of individuals?"

Diaz leaped into action. "Dr. Thorgason, this is a polite discussion among three people, mostly between you and Dr. Jones. There is no call for interrupting Dr. Jones, and I will not allow it to happen again."

Whit was overjoyed, even if he kept the feeling buried deep. Diaz was frank in his desire to muzzle him after he had rudely interrupted what Diaz perceived to be the more adult and more moral scientist at the table. But, by jumping into the fray and not, for instance, allowing Jones to defend himself, Diaz had left Whit's interruption echoing among watchers. Jones had begun his response by invoking his compassion, specifically concerning his mother's wintertime suffering. Nonetheless, the New Zealander's deep disdain for anything that could support Whit's side was so blinding that he had shown himself to be heartless for the second time in five minutes. It wasn't that Jones was unaware of the numbers Thorgason was presenting; as a physicist, Jones was a skilled mathematician who paid attention to all numbers associated with climate, whichever side proffered them in peer-reviewed articles. He privately considered Thorgason's point about wintertime mortality to be irrefutable. As Diaz finished needlessly defending him, he pondered how best to respond. So far, the event had proceeded in a hauntingly similar fashion to the debate in Auckland against the self-important comedian. If anything, tonight had gone worse; he was struggling to breathe.

"It takes a particular brand of arrogance," he said, "in the face of the warming of the atmosphere due to human emissions and all the problems associated with that, to claim that the real problem facing humankind is that it still gets cold in the winter. I'm speechless."

"Well, you've picked a good time for it," Diaz quipped, "because it's time for the first of our two breaks. We'll be right back."

A red light on the camera behind Whit's left shoulder went dark. The network, which naysayers had said would take a ratings hit with its pair of scientists arguing climate in primetime, was, after all, in the business of making money. Whit wondered what products were getting advertised as he and Jones strove to catch their breath. The director, Jessica Cahill, and the woman who had booked him, Erica, were suddenly at the table, standing to Diaz's right.

"Instant ratings are in," Erica said, to Diaz, but for Whit's benefit, too.

"The *truth* is monumental," Cahill said. "Like, Super Bowl monumental. Unprecedented."

"So, keep it up," Erica said.

"Thanks," Diaz said.

From the shadows behind the cameras on the scientists' side, an assistant director's voice half-shouted: "Sixty seconds."

When Diaz said, "We'll be right back," Whit had drunk his glass of water in four gulps.

Erica took note, called a production assistant over to refill Whit's glass, and announced: "You're doing well, gentlemen." There was a smile at the corner of her mouth, and Whit thought she had been looking his way while she spoke. Jones, who was so uncomfortable he had no idea whether he was thirsty, hungry, or anything else, picked up his water glass and took a sip. He had intended it as a gesture to show that he, too, was capable of drinking water, but even this hadn't gone well. As soon as the production assistant refilled Whit's glass, he drank two-thirds of it and smiled gratefully as the assistant filled it again. The assistant looked Jones's way, proffering the sweating pitcher of ice water as if to refill Jones's glass, but Jones raised the fingers of his right hand from the table in a no-thank you gesture.

"Ten seconds!" came the assistant director's voice from the shadows. Cahill, Nagle, and a few others milling around the table had disappeared. It was just the three participants again now.

"Five, four …," came the assistant director's voice, with the final three numbers being counted silently by the woman's hand reaching into the light from the shadows. Of the three at the table, only Diaz could see this, and only he needed to see.

23

We are back," Diaz said. "Dr. Jones, you mentioned the arrogance it takes, in your opinion, to say that people should be more concerned with some dying of hypothermia in their homes when most agree that global warming is imperiling the very planet upon which we live. And yet, the Fifty-Niners seem to be reaching a wide audience, and you have come here tonight yourself, breaking your moratorium against engaging with people like Dr. Thorgason. Did you honestly come here to reassure your mother?"

It was the closest that Diaz could come to spoon-feeding Jones, who had visibly done more damage to his side than he would have by refusing the invitation to come.

"If you knew Mum, you would take the issue of reassuring her more seriously," Jones quipped. Diaz smiled, and Whit nearly laughed himself. It was easy to forget the humanity of the people he had been fighting against for so long. "And I did not come here only to reassure her. But, Mum, if they put this on back home and you see it, thank you for making me curious enough about the world to become someone trying to save it. Your mind and curiosity made me the man I have become, for better or worse. But, Mum, don't let these people's suicides or their preoccupation with cold persuade you that your son has wasted his career or that any of us is safe from the gathering

storm that is global warming. Even the oil companies themselves agree with sounding alarm bells about warming, and they
have financed much of our research over the last twenty years. A
great time to be alive, Dr. Thorgason says. Well, I suppose it is,
compared to anyone born today who will inherit a world with
worse storms, worse droughts, worse floods, and higher sea levels than anything any of us have ever witnessed. In that sense
and that sense alone, now is indeed a great time to be alive. It is
easy for Dr. Thorgason and his horde to say that the authors of
the United Nations climate reports have it all wrong. It's all too
convenient to say that everything is a result of climate cycles
from here in an American television studio within a skyscraper.
I would point out that where hurricanes inflict their worst damage, you never find Dr. Thorgason or anyone of his ilk. Perhaps
that's because they know that their narrative about how normal
it is for your house to be ripped from its foundation is false.
Their narrative about how normal it is for your neighbors to lose
half their family members in a storm is false. Their stories about
how natural it is withstanding post-flooding cholera in the
twenty-first century are false. And the people who have gone
through these things might not take kindly to Dr. Thorgason
and the rest of the deniers at all, actually, and I'm not sure I'd
blame them for it."

Diaz did his best to cling to his role as an objective moderator. "Dr. Thorgason, your response?" he said in a near monotone.
But as a man who had made hay from destructive weather
throughout his career, Diaz couldn't hide his delight in Jones's
attack. Whether anyone at home registered the glee was uncertain, but Whit saw it.

"It is the year 2028," he began. "It has been twenty-five years
since I studied subglacial volcanoes during my doctoral work. If

you told me back then that another PhD scientist would some-day blame me for hurricanes on national television, as the most superstitious in our society have always blamed others for frightening weather, I wouldn't have believed you. But it just happened. Take a mental snapshot, America, because you are witnessing the retreat of human civilization from facts and logic to the disastrous belief systems that led humankind to burn tens of thousands of women as witches and to practice live human sacrifices atop pyramids. The hurricanes of the last several years, the ones that people at home know about, were tragic, frighten-ing, incredibly destructive, and much less so than the worst hur-ricanes on record, both in terms of lives lost and physical damage to coastlines. But no one at home watching this tonight can *see* those past storms in their minds. On the other hand, they can call up a few high-definition YouTubes of any of the hurricanes we've just gone through and watch the destruction play out, frame by frame, in super slow motion if they so desire, as some do. But that won't change the fact that blaming me or anyone else for hurricanes or other kinds of weather is fundamentally unscientific.

"We know, not only from the fact that sea level was higher in the past but from many other pieces of irrefutable evidence, that the ocean-atmosphere system is *not* in an unprecedented state. Indeed, it is nowhere near such a state. Our mistake toward the public as scientists has been frightening people out of using the most plentiful energy at our disposal as wisely as we possibly can. Our mistake is letting supposed scientists, such as the one who blamed me for a hurricane, obscure our vision of reality. And there is some hard reality that needs to be seen: for in-stance, that we built trillions of dollars' worth of infrastructure in the oceans' flood plain, not knowing when we did so what sea level had done last time the glaciers retreated." Though he had stowed his tape measure, Whit looked up calmly, to the point in space where the end of the tape had been just a few minutes before, and then continued. "We knew no better at the time; as human beings, we love water, and we need water to transport goods, and so, of course, we built infrastructure where the water was. But what scientists should be telling people is not, 'The water was always right next to where you built Miami Beach, and what is happening now is new and scary.' Scientists should be telling people, 'We're sorry; it was our responsibility to alert humanity as soon as we discovered that the sea level rises, all by itself, with no help from human-caused global warming. It rises to all sorts of places that will prove problematic, and here's what we can do to make it better now and prevent the worst from happening in the future.' That would be science. That would be useful. And that would be true."

Jones was confident that most people watching would have gotten lost in the weeds of Thorgason's response, and he couldn't help letting a faint smirk find its way into the corners of his mouth. Diaz was less confident that Thorgason had lost ground, but either way, the next question was for him.

"Dr. Thorgason, is it your position that humanity's use of fossil fuels has caused not a single death?"

"Thank you for asking me this," Whit said. "The public has never been told how many scientists dispute the global-warming narrative they see in the media day after day, week after week, month after month, year after year, and decade after decade. Terrifying weather and climate stories are a significant part of the media's bottom line, and people need to be clear about that. But, as for how scientists see climate, people need to understand that it has been impossible for honest debate to take place in academia for my entire professional life and before that. My presence here tonight means I will never have another grant approved, never be invited to speak at another conference. It means I will almost surely lose my position where I have been a faculty member for more than ten years and never get another comparable job for as long as I live. And nothing I have said tonight is anything but accurate and necessary. But so threatened have the people on Dr. Jones's side felt by any objections to their presentation of the climate narrative that they have attacked all dissenters, as we have already discussed, in the most personal terms. Believe me, if there isn't a silent majority who feel as Fifty-Niners feel about climate, there is a significant minority.

"But to honor the intention with which you ask me this question, I will say that industrial emissions may have warmed the atmosphere by half a degree or more compared to where it would be otherwise. And given that, it is certainly possible that some single weather event, be it a fire or a hurricane, has killed one more person than would have died in the absence of those emissions. But even as the atmosphere has gently warmed, it has done so within the parameters of past climate norms! When President Lincoln died in 1865, it was about the same time that a long period of cold climate change had made life on Earth significantly more lethal and less advantageous. Climatologists call the period the Little Ice Age. It's important to know that the Little Ice Age was rife with war, famine, and disease. We've been rebounding from it ever since, but we're still not as warm— if you look at where forests are in the Arctic, the size of glaciers, and many other measures—as we were seven thousand years ago. These are facts that no climatologist disputes.

"Warmth is better for humanity; it always has been and always will be. If a thousand more people died from hurricanes every year than they would without added heat-trapping gases in the atmosphere, which they most assuredly are not doing, that would be a tragedy. It also wouldn't begin to approach the far greater number who are dying now, like clockwork, because of the unnecessary fuel poverty that leads them not to keep themselves warm enough to survive."

"The humiliating and awful death of Dr. Jones's family friend from hypothermia is not an aberration, an anomaly, or a freak occurrence. It is, rather, the tiny tip of a large statistical iceberg that has been kept out of view of the public, at least those members of it lucky enough not to be suffering in dangerously cold homes themselves."

Jones had to bring to bear a great deal of willpower to obtain a physics PhD from the University of Auckland at the age of twenty-four. He had needed to apply even more to become chief of the most renowned climate science institution in the United States before he was forty. But still, the New Zealander was straining to find sufficient will as he inwardly repeated the mantra, *Do not roll your eyes; do not roll your eyes; do not roll your eyes.* The good news was that he succeeded. The bad news was that the effort not rolling his eyes was costing him was reflected in an unflattering grimace he wore on his face. It might have been better in the end to roll his eyes.

Diaz looked at Jones and had to pretend not to see what was happening on his contorted, straining face while addressing him again. "Dr. Jones, your response?"

"Fifteen of the warmest years ever recorded have occurred during the last two decades," Jones began. "Twelve of the most powerful twenty-five hurricanes ever measured have occurred since the turn of the century. China recently lost ten thousand men, women, and children to the Yellow River Flood. Glaciers are shrinking all over the globe. The most intense heatwaves ever recorded are happening almost every year now in Europe, South America, Asia, and, to a lesser extent, in the United States and Australia. The sea ice in the Arctic, commonly referred to as the world's air conditioner, has melted to the lowest levels ever witnessed during the satellite era. Credible scientific papers have been authored suggesting that one day in the not-too-distant future, climate refugees may need to colonize Antarctica, if not other planets, to survive this accelerating disaster that we call global warming. Neither I nor any other scientist involved in the worldwide effort to save us while there is still time invented the climate crisis. The climate crisis is occurring all around us, and those on my side are attempting to bring human behavior within more reasonable bounds in response to that crisis.

"Meanwhile, in Dr. Thorgason's world, it's always wintertime, with the most vulnerable among us succumbing to cold, like so many characters in a Dickens novel.

"Dr. Thorgason has told us that he is a father. Well, what kind of parent selects the fossil fuel industry as the recipient of his trust and goodwill, doing its bidding the same way he would if he were on its payroll? What kind of parent sacrifices the world his children stand to inherit to address what he perceives as an injustice suffered by his parents, themselves deniers, a generation ago? What kind of parent, indeed? Sea levels used to be higher than today, he tells us, and that is true. Therefore, we should put our heads in the sand as the seas rise now? That way, madness lies. And it is not just crazy; it is profoundly morally wrong. And, while the majority is not always right in scientific matters, it is most assuredly right in this case. The few holdouts, such as Dr. Thorgason and his crew of so-called Fifty-Niners, are like the lone survivors of World War II perched in palm trees on desert islands, waiting for the enemy to attack decades after the peace treaties were signed. The war is over, Dr. Thorgason, regarding the battle among scientists. Your side lost. But the battle for humankind's survival is on. And we could use your considerable intellect and passion on our side; will you not bring them to the effort?"

As Jones finished his response, he looked straight at Whit with what he hoped seemed genuine kindness. Whit knew that, if Jones managing not to roll his eyes had represented a superhuman effort on his part, generating what passed as sincerity while trying to lure him in with a cheap compliment was more challenging still. Whit had read Jones's words for more than twenty years, had observed him at the conference they'd both attended, had seen him on video countless times, and had now spent the better part of an hour with him. And there was one thing he knew about Jones beyond any shadow of a doubt: He and sincerity were not well acquainted. Jones was sly and indirect, as a matter of principle. The olive branch he held out was not what it appeared, not by a long shot.

Diaz, who looked reassured again, turned toward Whit with a look of mild disgust before giving him his turn. "Dr. Thorgason, your response?"

"Let me repeat it: I love nature, and I love this world," Whit said. "When it comes to Dr. Jones's assertions, I'll start by saying that ever is a big word, and forever is a long time. An early sign that Dr. Jones and the bulk of scientists on his side of the climate divide were trying to frighten people into supporting an agenda that is now freezing some to death in their homes was when they started using the word ever inappropriately. And that is just how he has used it tonight. Is Earth's temperature tonight the warmest ever? Far from it. Dr. Jones is well aware of this. But, for unknown reasons, he and his side have chosen to allow one hundred and fifty years of climate history to stand in for the tens of thousands of years that human beings have been on the globe. Using the word ever in this way is an insult to human intelligence, the intelligence of all the people watching this tonight, and mine personally as a scientist. Earth's average temperature, at this moment, is nowhere near the warmest it has ever been, absolutely nowhere near. But that won't stop Dr. Jones and his crew, well-intentioned or not, from using the words *warmest ever*, again and again. A real Nazi, Joseph Goebbels, said: 'If you tell a lie big enough and keep repeating it, people will eventually come to believe it.' The scariest part, to me, is that the people repeating the lie come to believe it themselves!

"Dr. Jones knows full well, as he knows that two plus two equals four and that gravity is non-negotiable, that now is not the warmest time in Earth's history. He knows this! They all know it, but another part of them has come to believe this lie they keep telling, and the lie relies on this one tiny but huge word: ever.

"Dr. Jones, is now the warmest time ever in Earth's climate history? I'm happy to give you a moment of my own time for this. Is it?"

"It . . . is . . . not," Jones said. Suddenly, the strain upon his face had gone, leaving him looking much younger, almost like a boy. "But—"

"Sorry, Dr. Jones, it was a yes-or-no question, and you have already answered it—truthfully," Whit said. "I give you vast credit for that. I know the professional risks you are taking by speaking honestly, and I know the personal cost that telling such a truth represents.

"Perhaps we can unburden your conscience a little further," Whit said. "Are the storms we are seeing the worst ever?"

"They ... are ... not," Jones said. His eyes turned red as years of pent-up emotion began to break free.

"Are forest fires the worst ever?"

"No," Jones said. A first tear came down his left cheek and disappeared in his long, bushy beard. Diaz was looking on in shock. Multiple producers were yelling at him to take back the reins of the discussion, but he knew, as a human being, if not as a journalist, that what was in the process of happening between the two scientists needed to play out.

"Is the ocean-atmosphere system on the brink of dangerous, runaway warming?"

"No, there are built-in buffers within the system that prevent it," Jones said. Tears were falling from both eyes, and his beard was becoming damp.

"Are the droughts of the past few decades worse than the megadroughts of the past two hundred thousand years?" Whit asked.

"Nowhere near as bad," Jones said. Tears streamed from his eyes; the ones he had first shed were now dripping from the bottom of his beard. The camera operators missed none of it.

The producers were so loud in Diaz's earpiece that Whit could hear the sound from across the table. "Go to break! Go to break!" the loudest of the voices said.

With what Whit thought was heroic calm, Diaz looked into the camera behind Whit's left shoulder and said, "We'll be right back for the final portion of our discussion." The light on the camera went off, and chaos ensued.

Erica Nagle and Jessica Cahill reappeared on set. Also appearing out of nowhere and milling about were several production assistants in headsets and a desperate-looking makeup artist tasked with restoring Jones's makeup after the deluge. Various executives in expensive suits clamored about the ratings touching a level none had previously seen. Three of the suited contingent, all men, had Cahill cornered; Whit could hear them lecturing her about not letting him and Jones continue in their suddenly peaceful ways. "Do you understand?" one of them asked her. His name was Richard Moynihan, a graduate of Columbia's business and journalism schools, one of her more oppressive bosses. With his $3,000 suit, $1,000 black loafers, salt-and-pepper hair in a $200 cut, and designer black-framed glasses, he was suddenly feeling less empowered than made any sense to him.

"I understand," Cahill said.

"Then make it happen," Moynihan said.

Cahill turned toward the table and took in that Whit, at least, had overheard Moynihan being belligerent and condescending to her. She looked Jones's way and saw that while the man was trying to stop shedding tears in deference to the makeup artist's work, he didn't appear to be putting his game face back on. Besides his beard, he looked like a seven-year-old boy after a long cry—positively cherubic. Whit's eyes reflected compassion, coupled with the fact that talking him into going for Jones's jugular for the sake of ratings was not going to be easy.

Cahill moved to the table, with the executives sidling close enough to eavesdrop. While prepared to be lectured publicly, in such extraordinary circumstances, she was unwilling to suffer the further indignity of being monitored by men who lacked the courage to do what they were asking her to do. "We're going to need some privacy," she told them, gesturing offstage with her eyes. As only seconds were left before the broadcast would resume, neither Moynihan nor any of the executive producers wasted time arguing. They knew their best hope lay in Cahill talking two men who had hated each other for decades into doing so for another twenty minutes. Moynihan, the most powerful of the execs who had taken the extraordinary step of storming the set, slipped into the shadows, trailed by the other well-heeled power players. Erica Nagle briskly walked into the shadows between another pair of cameras.

Cahill stepped beside Diaz and addressed Jones and Whit, emphasizing the one who had done all the crying. "You've picked a hell of a time to go kumbaya on us," she said. "Dr. Jones, it's hard to imagine that you have fully thought through the consequences of becoming a friend to the Fifty-Niners. Did you come to the studio tonight intending to give up your career? Because that's what's about to happen."

"Ten seconds," the assistant director's voice announced from the shadows.

"It's not too late," Cahill said, turning and departing from the stage.

24

Erica didn't know how she felt. She had come to have a grudging admiration for the Fifty-Niners, although even after her experiment and personal brush with cold's destructive power, she still felt they were extremists. Or, anyway, a part of her did. Another aspect of her was amazed by what Thorgason had just achieved in the first two-thirds of the debate. It was as though he had performed a kind of exorcism or, at the very least, a religious conversion.

When she had stood nearby the debate table during the executives' remonstrations of Cahill and then Cahill's plea to the scientists to return to mutual hostility, the relief coming from Jones was palpable. And this conversion had taken place in a man who was profoundly reluctant to experience such a thing. But it had happened, and during her brief moments in his vicinity during the break, it seemed to Erica that Jones radiated serenity from such a deep place that she wondered if he would even be willing to speak during the final segment.

"Is your résumé in shape?" a voice beside her asked. It was Rita Guzman. Erica was so lost in thoughts about the debate she hadn't noticed Guzman drawing near. Guzman's passive-aggressive bomb, typical of her, was beautifully calculated. After all, she could plausibly assert the question was asked out of collegiality. The status of Erica's résumé had already crossed her mind more than once; she was no fool. But even if it came down to that, today was not the day.

"I'm not sure we're to that point yet," she said. "But I appreciate your concern."

"I'd be touchy, too," Guzman said, walking away before Erica could attempt any response.

This had all taken place during the ten seconds before the debate went back on the air. Everyone on staff at *The Nightly News* was well capable of compacting social interactions, as necessary, into the microscopic pieces of time that live television left them. With Guzman having accomplished what she set out to accomplish, Erica now watched as the assistant director's hand counted down for the third and last time: *three, two, one.*

25

Erica was not alone in her confusion among those watching the debate. There were all kinds of reactions among the viewing public in different places worldwide, with rage, disappointment, curiosity, and joy finding expression, too.

In the United States, MSNBC and NBC News provided the debate through both their broadcast arms and their online platforms. In Concepcion, Chile, Juanita Tagawa watched on MSNBC.com in her loft. The Southern Hemisphere's winter solstice—June 21—was less than a month away, and the weather outside her darkened windows was raw. With fog, drizzle, and a temperature of 48 degrees, it wasn't unlike the weather in the U.K. when Gertie invisibly passed.

Juanita knew nothing of this woman on the other side of the world, not specifically, but through some recent research, she had become an expert in cold's effects on the body. It was one of the ways she had of missing Miguel less, of honoring the sacrifice he had made for humanity. Although becoming a Fifty-Niner might never be her choice, it was clear to her that he and his friends had right on their side in this horrifying conflict with the Climatists. And she knew many, even in her relatively mild country, died annually due to the skyrocketing cost of energy. Though no one was with her in her loft as she watched on her couch with a glass of red wine, she was, in fact, not watching the debate alone. Whit's wife, Amy, suggested they maintain a video call between them in their separate homes. For Juanita, it meant using her laptop to watch the debate and her phone for her video connection with Amy. In return for the small effort it cost her, she beheld a friendly face beamed through the internet from Boulder, registering many of the same emotions of stern courage, surprise, and amazement that she knew were finding their way onto her own. Neither spoke much. The occasional "wow" and "whoa" were about all they said. Still, their connection transformed the experience of watching from one that might have been lonely to one that wasn't.

When Jones began to weep in the last few minutes before the second break, they opened their mouths in silent amazement.

When the second commercial break had begun, they conversed more freely.

"I'm sure that's going to be bad for Jones and the rest on his side, but I'm not sure it's going to be great for us," Amy said.

"Because people will blame Whit for Jones's tears?" Juanita asked.

"Exactly," Amy said. "Jones wept because of being lured into being honest, and I don't think people will focus on the honesty."

"Because they'll think Whit manipulated him into it?" Juanita said.

"Didn't he?" Amy said.

"I'm not convinced it's possible to manipulate a scientist into crying using mere words."

"But you're a subtle woman with a refined intellect," Amy said.

"You got to know me fast!" Juanita said, laughing.

"It is funny, but it may also prove to be terrible news, more terrible news, for my family," Amy said.

"Some may blame Whit, and some may not," Juanita said. "But everyone will see the relief that the true answers, and the tears, brought Jones. As I have studied Miguel's work more seriously since his death, I have come to think of this Dr. Jones as an awful person, if I may speak seriously. But even I was moved by what he showed. That must be good for Whit and us, no?"

"I hope so," Amy said. "I don't think so, but I hope so."

"The commercial is ending," Juanita said.

"I don't have a good feeling," Amy said.

The two, separated by five and a half thousand miles and two time zones, settled in to watch the last segment. Amy, who only prayed in emergencies, did so now.

26

Windsor Communications was in crisis mode. Having produced the best-selling books attributed to climate scientists for thirty years, the team had been furious over the Fifty-Niners' success in swaying public opinion, if only marginally, over the previous six months. It had been the aging founder of the company, James Windsor, who had insisted that Jones debate Thorgason. No one else had thought it was a good idea initially. But the old man's record across the decades was one of triumph followed by triumph. Windsor kept a low profile but had, with his communications products, personally brought tens of millions of people down the path of climate change concern from vague discomfort to radicalized despair. Windsor, and his minions, had feathered the nest for Climatists at NBC News from the beginning, and Windsor was confident that Jones, no matter what he might lack in terms of spine, would never lose a second public debate.

When it became apparent during the broadcast that Jones was doing precisely that, Windsor felt reassured that he had insisted that the entire New York team be in the office two hours before the debate. They had been watching together in the larger of the firm's two conference rooms. Eighteen PR professionals sat around the table. Each could win an argument about humanity's need to shrink its carbon footprint drastically in the next few years. And yet each had visited an average of three continents, and their jet travels never ceased. Collectively, their destinations included every European capital; every Asian capital; every South American capital; every city larger than 500,000 people in Australia; all fifty U.S. states; more than a dozen Polynesian islands, including Tahiti; the Himalayas; the Swiss Alps; the German Alps; the Austrian Alps; the French Alps; the Italian Alps; Antarctica; Iceland; Greenland; the Caribbean; two-thirds of the countries in Africa; and Beijing, Tokyo, and Hong Kong (among many other Asian cities).

Windsor himself was the most astonishing contributor to the list of destinations, the most frequent flier. As the son of a Houston oil family who had cut his teeth as a PR flack working for the company of one of his father's industry friends in the early 1970s. Windsor had experienced a change of heart when it came to Big Oil after his employer's daughter, to whom Windsor was engaged to be married, turned out to have been sleeping with two of his closest friends, who happened to be work associates. It had suddenly seemed to the young Windsor that everyone involved with the industry was a despicable snake, a feeling that never left him. The psychological crisis had been the first step toward his becoming an influence-wielding leftist. That had been in 1973 when he happened to be smoking a fair amount of pot. He was pretty close to unmoored for years afterward, hanging out at music venues around South Texas, and promoting a few bands along the way. By 1980, however, he had been sufficiently radicalized by counter-culture friends and had found his PR groove as a leftist communications guru. Born into privilege, it was now clear to Windsor that The Man was the problem.

Further, modern industrial civilization was the worst thing to have happened to humankind; the sincerity with which he held his views and a sharp mind that somehow grew more powerful during his hippie years provided him with a sort of magic in the realm of PR. It turned out that influential people around the country and the globe felt the same way he did about how civilization was structured. And it turned out he possessed a gift for providing them with PR products they found singularly valuable. But he never lost the taste for jet travel that he had acquired flying to holiday destinations with his family as a boy. Among his favorite trips was flying annually on private jets to the self-styled world-savers forum at Davos, Switzerland. It was among the only places left on Earth where his light-brown eyes didn't sicken him when he saw them in his hotel mirror.

As Jones answered Thorgason's series of simple questions in the worst possible ways, the swearing around the conference table was epic, led by Windsor himself.

"God, f'ing damn it," Windsor said when Jones's first tears escaped his eyes. "Weak-tit motherfucker!" Beyond swearing, no one spoke during the debate itself, but by the time the second break came, it was plain steps would need to be taken.

"You are freaking kidding me," said Rick Peabody. Like more than half the people around the table, he had Ivy League degrees and offered psychological cover and intellectual firepower to the brilliant but informally educated Windsor.

"He thinks he's Jesus," Windsor said of Jones. "He thinks this debate is his cross."

"Um," said Priya Bhatt, the PhD daughter of an Indian diplomat, who had been with the firm since graduating from Stanford, "isn't he famously Buddhist?"

"Your point?" Windsor said, flashing her a venomous look. "We'll need a statement for him before the 10 o'clock news on the East Coast. Richard and Priya, you're feeling talkative. Get this down: He was on a new medication today and has been under extraordinary stress. He takes saving the world from the deniers' evil schemes to heart, which has weakened him. He has avoided the public eye until now because he is a scientist's scientist."

"But we've sent him on the road supporting books we wrote in his name," Bhatt dared to add. "That's not avoiding the public eye, right?"

"Does Jones look like someone who developed a spine of steel while dealing with the public?" Windsor asked. "The story fits the man. Are you confused about that?"

"The break is ending," Peabody said. "I assume you want us to watch the last part of the debate before we start drafting this?"

"I've already drafted it for you just now; you'll merely be typing," Windsor said. "But, yes, of course. We all need to see what happens. I never wanted him to head GISS."

The fact that Windsor had had a say about who became head at Goddard Institute for Space Studies, NASA's climate bureau, gently settled over the room; no one spoke for a few seconds.

When the commercial ended, and Frederick Diaz's face reappeared, Windsor directed everyone's eyes to the TV with his own. And that's when things went from a little weird to very weird.

27

Jones had no idea how he might survive the last segment of the debate. Having shed so many tears during the previous part, he had only one priority: not to cry. Jones felt a strong affinity for Thorgason, understanding that the volcanologist had liberated him sufficiently to taste tears that possessed grace. At the same time, he was furious with Thorgason for humiliating him, which he knew was how most would interpret his breakdown.

Whit had a plan for the segment, but he wasn't sure how to put it to use. He had achieved more than he had thought possible, and he didn't want to appear to run any victory laps before the event was over. His first goal was to establish that he knew Jones's meltdown was an act of courage, one beneficial for Jones but also humanity. Still, there were points to be made and only limited time. To his surprise, he felt more pressure at the start of the last segment than in the green room or any other point all day.

Diaz felt about as much uncertainty as the two debaters. Already the night had changed the narrative of his career. A high-profile event, even if the *truth* came down from its recent heights during the most recent segment, he understood that the bulk of his peers would do anything to be associated with ratings like these for a news event, no matter how bizarre the occasion was. Producers were speaking in his ear as he came back on the

air, feeding him the same directive the executives gave Cahill—
to reignite the battle between the scientists. It wasn't as if he
wouldn't have known it on his own.

"And we're back," he said. "Dr. Thorgason, traditionally, scientists stayed out of political debates. But you have assembled a
team of suicide PhD's to attempt to change our course as a society away from renewables and back to dirty fossil fuels, presumably. In the process, tonight, you have somehow succeeded in
getting one of the leading lights of science to lose track of his
core principles. I am sure many at home are wondering, do you
get a paycheck from the fossil fuel industry? And, if so, do you
feel good about that?"

"It's good to talk about the corrupting influence of money on
science, specifically climate science," Whit began calmly, to Diaz's disappointment. "First, let me answer your question: No, I
have never received any funds from anyone other than my university and the funders of my various grants, none of whom have
anything to do with the fossil fuel industry, and all of whom, by
the way, are no doubt regretting their choosing me as their grant
recipient tonight. But you're right that money corrupts climate
science and not in the way that the public thinks.

"There's some idea among the public that the oil and coal
companies have funded scientists to falsify their findings in the
same way that Big Tobacco was able to cloak itself in a veneer of
science before the public learned the truth about it. Corporate
malfeasance like that isn't the case with climate, not in any sub-
stantive way. I researched this exhaustively and found a handful
of scientists who had accepted speaking fees from the fossil
fuel industry for a few thousand dollars and travel stipends to
cover lodging and travel to speak. Meanwhile, Big Oil alone has
spent lavishly supporting the climate narrative. Big Oil dollars

reinforced the public's sense that sea level used to be stable, that the warmest temperature in a hundred and fifty years constituted the warmest temperature ever, and that floods and droughts used to be less devastating—none of which is true. Big Oil has contributed billions, with a 'B,' supporting this narrative because it thought it *had* to. And it felt it had to because the United States government, the United Nations, universities, and journalists all over the world coalesced around this idea of a climate crisis. Whether or not you think that's an intentional conspiracy, the simple truth is that climate science funding has been traveling in a single direction for more than forty years!

"But before giving Dr. Jones his chance to respond, let me return to your direct question. Please understand that allying myself with the Fifty-Niners, and, yes, helping the group come into existence will have cost me any future career in the science that I love. So, while I, as the father of children whom I would never abandon by letting Earth's fifty-nine-degree temperature claim me, in the way my friends have courageously done, I am committing career suicide by being here tonight. And so, no, I'm not profiting from informing the public of a few simple facts about climate, including the crucial information that hundreds of thousands of individuals die of cold in their homes each year. Just the opposite, I am paying a high price for telling you and everyone at home the truth tonight."

When Whit finished, Jones looked as uncertain as he had at the end of the break; Diaz mostly looked annoyed.

"Doctor Jones?" he said, managing to flash the scientist a warm look in hopes the man might buck up.

"Physics and math can be harnessed to support nearly any position on climate," Jones said, "and I never especially liked either. My mum did, on my behalf. 'The world will always need a man good at maths,' she said. Meanwhile, my dad whispered in my ear from my earliest days that capitalism was perverse. If left the chance, I would have preferred laboratory science. I would have done anything to get to measure things. Yes, my NASA predecessors manipulated the temperature record for Reykjavik, and I have done so for other stations. There were sound mathematical reasons for doing so. But in my case, altering a historical temperature record was the closest I could come to *measuring* temperature directly, personally, which my training and career path kept me from doing. The truth is that scientists have barely any idea what Earth's average temperature is. That's partly because we have so few measuring stations, partly because so few of those stations have been in pristine, unchanged conditions since their initial installation, and partly because the idea of averaging temperature is an unphysical, unscientific thing to do.

"You're probably better off using sea level as a global thermometer, and sea level has been increasing in tiny increments, with pauses, for seven thousand years. It doesn't make a solid headline, does it? But this business of 'warmest ever'"—he raised two fingers with each hand to form air quotes—"it makes a world-class headline. Journalists floated the word originally out of desperation to sell newspapers in a world that increasingly didn't want them. Scientists on my side immediately saw how powerful the words were. 'Warmest ever,' 'warmest ever,' 'warmest ever,' we said, and the newspapers couldn't believe their luck. They had distorted our science while selling it to a gullible public, but now we were distorting it for them, doing their work for them. And they could say that it wasn't them saying it, that it was us, even though we were quoting them when they misquoted us. It's a freak show.

"The words 'warmest ever' to describe any year that we have been alive are laughable, but what they have been used to achieve is tragic. I've known about people dying in their homes, and I have known that my actions helped lead to this situation. But, for whatever reason, the full truth of it has come to me tonight. And I won't be a party to it. If you're going to take this man, who has more of a scientist in him than ninety-nine percent of those on my side, and take away his career, then you had better do the same to me. I'm done lying. I'm done bullying people to make my parents right and myself miserable. I'm done."

Diaz, who had forgotten he was hosting a debate for a moment, stared at Jones as though he were watching a comet wipe out a city. He was, in the truest sense of the word, dumbfounded. The squawking of producers once again emanated from his earbud loudly enough for Whit and Jones to hear.

"Dr. Jones," he said, "are you resigning your position at NASA?"

"I think it's his turn," Jones said, gesturing to Thorgason with a lift of his chin.

"It's actually your turn to answer a debate question, but I would just like to ask before posing that: Are you resigning your position at NASA?"

"I've just told you," Jones began, "that I am part of the greatest conspiracy of the last thousand years, one designed to dismantle the western economic system, and by extension, the western political system, meaning democracy; and that I did nothing to stop the changing of the temperature record for a vitally important station in Iceland, as well as those of hundreds of other stations, in order to make the global mean temperature appear to be rising in a way that we could reasonably call 'unprecedented,' even if that was only true for the last century and a half, a pathetically short period when it comes to anything having to do with climate; and that mathematics has been used to support this conspiracy in ways that are morally repugnant; and that the man with whom I am supposedly arguing tonight is a man of extraordinary integrity, both scientifically and personally; and that the idea that he cannot even have a career in science, after more or less sacrificing his future prospects on an altar of concern for his fellow humanity is so hideous that I will not allow it to happen, if there is anything I have to say about it; and all you can do is ask is, am I am resigning? Do you understand how your question obscures a profoundly important set of revelations placed on the table here, as it were, right before your eyes? And all you can do is shrink down this conspiracy and this brutalization of millions of the poor and elderly through unnecessary fuel poverty to the question of one man's job at NASA? Are you daft? I'm asking you, seriously—are you daft?"

"I'm taking that as a 'no,'" Diaz said. "I'm sure I'm not the only one confused by your sudden change of heart. Can you put your decision in greater context?"

"My heart has not changed on any of this in a long time," Jones began. "When I was in high school, I was as worried about global warming as any good Labour family schoolboy in New Zealand. Those deemed gifted in maths and science were given special indoctrination at the time. It was the mid-1980s. And I did legitimately think the world was headed to hell in a handbasket because of human emissions of carbon dioxide; it was explained to me very clearly and convincingly by special tutors hired for the purpose. And then, strong-armed by my parents in different ways, I progressed through my academic training, with a strong leftward tilt guiding me all the while. And though I didn't particularly enjoy completing the PhD in physics that I received from the University of Auckland, it couldn't have gone any better for me. It hurt me, in retrospect, I see now not to be pursuing my life's passion, which was non-abstract science. But it also took the pressure off me. I used my maths training to be close to science and specifically as close to climate science as I could. It turned out that I was a genius for manipulating temperature records and 'averaging' them"—he made the air quotes once more—"and that people driving the climate crisis narrative were other people like me. We were, with few exceptions, maths guys. We were never, ever going to be spending our lives being wined and dined around the world and having microphones shoved in our faces and books written in our names with royalties going into *our* bank accounts as if we had truly written them. The only way that would ever happen was if we were part of a Trojan-horse assault on capitalism made possible by the average citizen's absolute loathing for anything having to do with science. Mr. Diaz, you're an esteemed journalist, and you have made climate change a central part of your career, or else you wouldn't have been selected as the moderator here tonight. Am I right? And would you mind telling the people at home how many peer-reviewed scientific articles you have read, personally, during your entire lifetime?"

Diaz looked at Jones in angry silence.

"I don't mean to pick on you, just the opposite," Jones said. "Like most journalists, you say you love science and believe it, but you don't *actually* love science. And, to that extent, you're like your colleagues covering this subject and even more like everyone home watching tonight. The louder people say they love science and want to protect it, the less likely it is that they have studied it, even for a few minutes, after completing their compulsory education.

"I've known that all the deception, by others and myself, made me sick for my entire tenure as the most influential single climate scientist in the United States. But I'm as human as anyone, and I knew that by continuing in my career, I was making my mum happy and would have been making my dad happy if he hadn't died the year before I went to college. Along the way, I flew to dozens of destinations as others told me I was the savior of humankind and of the earth itself. And I was making a better income than the pay of most of my family in New Zealand bundled together. But no, my heart did not change tonight. For the first time, I just decided to show someone other than myself what it contained."

"Still want to ask me that question?" Jones asked.

Diaz had put back on his mask, his eyes reflecting the piercing intellect for which he was known within the public.

"So, the environment is in great shape then, according to you, Dr. Jones? And should we continue to pollute it as much as we can? Do I have that about right?"

"What the Russians and the Chinese are doing to the environment is very serious," Jones said. "What the Indians are doing to the environment is serious. We have environmental movements in the West that were necessary when they started, which will be necessary for a very long time, and which have been enormously successful, by and large, thank God. Most of the rivers and lakes in the West are dramatically less polluted than when my grandparents were born. Most communities in the West, although unfortunately not all, have dramatically cleaner air than they did when my parents were born. Life expectancy and quality of life by all objective measures continue to increase. And it's all attributable to the environmental movement, which had its first significant stirrings in London during the 1950s.

But on the heels of westerners' improving how we manage our water and air, the environmental movement has become extreme in its methods. It would put a chokehold on normal economic activity here while turning a blind eye to what is happening in the countries I just mentioned. It's unclear whether anything good has come from the global warming movement. If there's one thing, it may be people's capacity to envision our planet as a single entity. It is important to remember that we are one species on one planet with one chance at getting this right. But killing people like my mother's friend with fuel poverty is not getting this right, not by a long way. I'm all for a Manhattan Project–style effort to develop legitimate forms of sustainable energy to make it possible for Russia, China, and India to lower their emissions and for us to get even better at cleaning up our side of the street. But I'm not for pretending we have fifteen years—or fifteen months—to eliminate fossil-fuel emissions. I'm not for pretending each of us is like a heroine strapped to a railway bed in a silent movie as seawater rises over our noses and drowns us en masse. That I am not for, and no honest scientist is."

Diaz's face registered disgust as Jones brought his response to a close. The night had been both the best and the worst of his career, and he was having trouble controlling his thoughts.

"Dr. Thorgason, your response?" he asked in the most neutral voice possible.

"My response is this," Whit said, "Fifty-Niners, desist. As moved as I am by Dr. Jones's noble example, I see tonight from the vantage point of this television network what should have been clear to me long ago: We cannot win. Even if dozens more scientists on our side took their lives in fifty-nine-degree death chambers, we would not win. Even if hundreds did so, we would not win. I see tonight that the forces arrayed against us are more powerful than I could understand before coming here."

A producer spoke in Diaz's ear: "The *truth* is beautiful."

"In many ways," Whit went on, "this is not only a battle between the righteous and the unrighteous but a battle between the silent and the articulate, between the invisible and the visible among us, between the meek and the less meek. As I witness the tremendous power of just a single television news network and realize that this is but one of many such armies arrayed against those on my side, it is clear we cannot win. We may have small victories, such as tonight's, but we cannot win. There will be skirmishes still, but the war, a war against needless suffering and death among the weakest of us, is lost. Just ask James Windsor." With that, he pulled the earbud from his ear, strode the step and a half to Jones's seat with his hand extended, shook the stunned Jones's hand while saying "Thank you," and stepped from the stage into the darkness.

The moment Whit had gone, producers roared in Diaz's ear. So far as he had known until then, he only had two producers, both women. But there was a man's voice in his ear, and with all three speaking over one another, it was impossible to understand. He thought he heard, "keep Jones talking…question, ask him a question…does he regret taking the side of someone who would…Windsor." Whit had been out of sight for five seconds or less. Diaz and Jones remained silent as Diaz tried to understand what his producers were saying. To the crew, the dead airtime felt like three minutes. The camera operator, who had been tight on Whit's face, zoomed out, not having Whit as a subject for his lens any longer, and his shot now captured Diaz's back, Whit's empty chair, and Jones's alarmed and confused expression. Jones had taken Whit's outstretched hand in his own, and there was no mistaking the admiration on his face as the two shook hands. When Whit was gone, Jones's eyes expressed confusion and abandonment.

However, Diaz hadn't earned the seat in which he sat by being easily rattled, and he pretended Jones's rough treatment of him had never occurred. "Dr. Jones," he said, again flashing the bewildered New Zealander all the reassurance he could, "you are to be commended for lasting until the end of the debate." While arguably condescending, the remark was also fair enough, and it did bring Jones's mind back to the problem at hand: debating a man who was no longer at the table with them. "Have you ever met James Windsor? And do you know why Dr. Thorgason would speak his name and leave the way he just did?"

"Don't do it," Windsor said from his spot in his firm's conference room.

"I—" Jones stammered.

"Don't do it," Windsor repeated, his face a twisted mask of rage. Staff on his team, from the lowest to the highest rung, were exchanging furtive looks as they watched the old man display fear none of them had ever witnessed in him.

"My books—" Jones said, pausing as he sought courage. Diaz looked at him with what could only be called tenderness, the type a compassionate father directs toward his son when he needs support.

"Don't you fucking dare!" Windsor said, a speck of saliva escaping his mouth. And now, the trusted members of the team he had assembled over the previous four decades worried not only for his future but for their own. The old man was losing it. And it was apparently not going to be pretty. Some of them intuited that the firm had authored more than half the major climate science books to make the bestseller lists, including Jones's three works. What no one in the room knew except the old man, however, was that the ghostwriter for Jones was Windsor himself. For reasons, his authorship was knowledge he didn't want to have disseminated—not to his staff and even less to a national TV audience.

Diaz, all too aware that this would not end the way he or his producers would have chosen, prompted Jones again: "Your books?"

At this, Jones removed his earpiece, stood, and hurried surprisingly quickly into the darkness and out of the studio. The competing voices had reached such a crescendo in Diaz's ear that he had no choice if he wanted to manage a closing remark amid the mayhem. He removed his earbud, looked toward the camera with its red light illuminated, and said, "Thank you for tuning in to what will certainly be one of the most talked about debates on climate. I am Frederick Diaz; good night."

28

Unlike most watching the debate, Juanita and Amy thought it might be a good sign when Whit suddenly shook Jones's hand and disappeared. While people who were in the habit of taking their news without a side dish of skepticism saw a man who had given up on his life's work run from the soundstage, the two women, one who knew Whit well and one who merely knew about him, saw a man with a plan. Neither of them knew what it might be, but they were confident that this was far from the end for the Fifty-Niners or Whit.

And it was not.

Windsor didn't stop to wonder whether or not Thorgason had a plan; he was going to destroy him—and the rest of the Fifty-Niners. Climatism was not merely about frightening people, after all. It was about controlling them, and the situation was out of control.

When Windsor had first heard about the idea that humankind could imperil the planet with industrial emissions of various sorts, it had been during his private, hazy experience of the 1970s. Amid several three-foot bongs in a tapestry-enshrouded smoking parlor that happened to be his living room, his life had changed. It had happened without his realizing when he saw a climate scientist from Stanford interviewed on television in an episode of a sci-fi documentary series. The scientist, Russell

Bender, with images of a recent bitter mid-Western winter flickering in the background, made a convincing case that the cold weather plaguing humankind for the past few decades had resulted from human activity. It was part of what became known later as the global-cooling scare. Windsor, feeling both high and clear-minded, wasn't scared by what the scientist was saying. He was confident it would never get cold outside his door in the Houston suburbs, no matter what humankind did. It made no difference to him if the scientist he had seen was right or wrong, or insane, for that matter, which it appeared he probably was. What Windsor understood all at once was this: Scientists possessed a singular ability to manipulate people with fear.

Within three years, Windsor had started his influential, left-leaning communications agency in New York City. Startlingly, during the same three-year period, Bender had changed his view 180 degrees. Human activity was *not* on the verge of freezing everyone to death, he and his colleagues now held. Instead, the human race was on the verge of changing the climate in unprecedented and dangerous ways through a process known as global warming. Windsor didn't care one way or the other. Cooling, warming, it was all the same to him. He just needed people to receive a good initial dose of fear from a source they trusted, and he would do the rest.

From his earliest days at his firm, Windsor was intent on using scientists to help him pull the U.S. government and the country as far to the left as far as he could. Bender was the first individual whom he called to get the work started. The man, as Windsor had suspected, was enormously flattered by the things Windsor told him, most notably that Bender was one of only a handful of men in the world with the vision to save humanity from itself and that Windsor could help him fulfill his destiny.

It took Windsor until the late 1980s to assemble the team of climate scientists he considered his own. In addition to Bender at Stanford, he had one at the University of Virginia, one at Yale, one at Columbia, one at MIT, one at UCLA, and one at Berkeley. All told, there were seven on the initial version of the team (it would later grow). Each was brilliant; each was instantly on board to do everything within his power to change the narrative on climate science. It needed alteration from that of an intellectual discipline in its infancy, characterized by insufficient data and mutually reinforcing uncertainties, to one with a single clear message: tailpipes and smokestacks were turning the world into a stormy hellhole.

The science team assembled, and his agency up and running, Windsor could scarcely believe his good fortune. He placed story after story presenting catastrophic global-warming scenarios in the *New York Times*, the *Washington Post*, and the other still-viable newspapers around the country at the time. As with the scientists he came to produce books for, the success of the narrative was closely linked to his own—personally, professionally, and financially. He was far from the only one to foresee a future in which Climatism would reign supreme among all news stories. Peers and competitors touting the same ideas existed at universities, think tanks, other communications firms, governments, and the United Nations. The U.N. was, before long, bankrolling scientific reports to the tune of hundreds of millions of dollars. But Windsor was singularly successful in creating a nexus between players in the Climatism drama; indeed, he was the nexus in many ways.

By the time Whit, Mike O'Brien, and Dema Choedrak came up with the idea of what would become the Fifty-Niners during their Antarctic research trip, Windsor had seen himself transition from a stoned, South Texas radical to one of the most powerful men in the world. And compared to the people with whom he competed for influence—among them, members of the British royal family—he was nearly anonymous. And that was how Windsor liked it. Indeed, his ability to sway public opinion relied on the fact that he had successfully put scientists' résumés and faces into the public eye, but not his own. It had been an incredible run. But now, close to the finish line of his outstanding career, hearing his name mentioned on national television by a man he instantly considered his mortal enemy was too much to bear; it could not stand.

"Rick, Priya: statement, ten minutes," he said.

"I'm not sure the medication and stress and media-virgin thing is going to work," Peabody said.

"I'm not sure he'll accept a phone call," Bhatt said, "with all due respect."

"He would not dare refuse my call," Windsor said.

"The old Jones wouldn't. That's true," Peabody said.

"There is no new Jones," said Windsor, "and there will never be a new Jones."

"Time is wasting," Bhatt said. "What if we took a less aggressive tack with him? He already seems gun shy."

"Go on," Windsor said.

"'Nigel, I'm sorry I put you in that situation. I can make it up to you. Call me,'" Bhatt said.

"Send that," Windsor said. He had four iPhones, two of which he managed on his own and two that were managed partly by staff and partly by himself. Even Jones, he knew, had more than one number.

"Send it to his phone marked 'private-private' in my contacts," Windsor said. "Everyone but Priya and Rick to their offices.

We're going to be in here for the night."

It was evident to all the staff that they were on a wartime footing now.

"Delivered, read. No response," Bhatt said.

"'Where can I meet you?'" Windsor said. "Send that."

"Are you sure?" Bhatt asked.

"I'm sure."

29

Hustling along the sidewalk, Jones had no intention of listening to the voicemails or reading any of the dozens of texts received while his phone was off. He wasn't sure he would ever use a phone again at all. He felt free in a way he hadn't since he was young. *The truth will set you free*, people always told him.

Yes, it will, he thought. *And, yes, it has.*

He was walking in the direction of Sixth Avenue, where he had an Uber arriving in two minutes. Striding toward the curb and noticing the beauty of the evening sky for the first time in what seemed like a long time, he found he was experiencing something he had only heard described and always doubted: ecstasy. It came to him that it had never been modernity or the threats posed by terrorism, technology, or violent criminals that had made his own body feel so heavy for the last couple of decades. He saw now that the weight had come from his thoughts, the lies he had digested, or, more accurately, swallowed, and the lies he had told. The world was a beautiful place, enshrouded with holy mysteries, and being alive, right now was a tremendous privilege. And it would only get better.

He had decided that even if Thorgason's people obeyed the command to halt their efforts to save the world with their videos, there would be at least one more: his own.

Having spent his adult life until now wedded to his education and then his career, he would be leaving no spouse or children behind. And that made the decision even more joyful.

His mother and colleagues would miss him; a few people with whom he played the occasional game of squash might miss him. But all of them and the rest of the world would see that he was no mere theoretical physicist. He was a scientist who measured things and understood that any scientific measurement of *his* effect on the planet would show he had contributed to the silent holocaust described by Thorgason at the debate. He was, of course, talented at math. The fuel poverty from "green energy" had been a concern, if not an obsession, before his mother brought him the news of the family friend's hypothermic death. And anyone who looked at the exploding energy costs associated with the unrestrained rush to wind and solar power could not help but see (if they were honest) that Climatism had claimed more lives than it had ever saved or ever would.

As his luxury Uber made its way uptown along Central Park West per his self-indulgent request (Amsterdam Avenue would have been faster and cheaper for arriving at Columbia), he reviewed the tools he needed for the video. First, there was his building's HVAC system. Though it became temperamental about every eighteen months, requiring expensive and annoying repairs during which everyone was miserable, it had just been fixed and was working well. All other buildings on Columbia's campus that he was aware of had tiny temperature ranges that their thermostats controlled. Still, an administrator during the early 2000s had decided GISS personnel would be able to control the temperature of their space, free from the draconian constraints.

Generally speaking, the system kept the institute at the same temperature as the surrounding buildings on Columbia's Morningside Heights campus. But someone had successfully argued that the institute might need one day to create a broader range of conditions on-site to recreate various temperature-measuring issues in the field. Jones knew that the thermostat would do his bidding because he had jacked it up and down when working alone late at night to ensure it functioned.

As for recording his vital signs, that was not something he could do much about. There was no possibility of hooking himself up as the real Fifty-Niners had done. But what the video lacked in terms of technical sophistication, it would make up for in terms of shock value; that was his hope. He had the Uber drop him in front of a Duane Reade Pharmacy between 111th Street and 112th Street, where he ran in to purchase a standard home thermometer and three fans. It made him giddy to know that he would be measuring temperature, even in such a humble way, in the last few hours of his life. Standing in line at the register with the Braun ThermoScan7 thermometer and three Lasko fans, it flitted through Jones's mind that his evening was quite different from that of anyone else in the store. He also felt the same happiness he had known walking from Rockefeller Center to his Uber pickup. After paying, the thought that someone would dig up the video taken of him by the Duane Reade security cameras led him to face the camera above the door and present what might have been the widest smile of his life.

He felt self-conscious, suddenly, getting his key in the door of the building housing the institute, but once he had the fans, the Duane Reade bag, and himself inside, he felt comfortable again. He shuffled to the elevator, pushed the call button, and felt relief and satisfaction as the doors opened. He stepped in the car, pushed the button for the sixth floor, and whispered "yes" to himself in triumph as the doors closed. As he was expecting, the sixth floor had no one working on it. Several staff members were likely working at home, but after 8 P.M., you could bet you would have the whole institute to yourself. It was a luxury he allowed himself every so often, and tonight he would enjoy it deeply. He strode to his office door, unlocked it, stepped inside, and closed the door behind him. Then he walked to the thermostat and set it at fifty-nine degrees.

He crossed the room, lay the Duane Reade bag holding the thermometer and all three fans on his desk, closed his window blinds, and stripped down to his underwear, taking care to remove his socks. He had promised himself that he would begin playing squash more regularly a decade before, and he had even made it to the courts in the Columbia gym twice a week, three different times. For five years, though, the bulk of the exercise he got was walking to and from work, the grocery store, and a Chinese restaurant he favored. He had, at an optimistic moment some number of years earlier (three? or four? he couldn't remember), put a duffel bag with gym clothes in a small closet that came with the office. He now took out shorts and a Columbia-light-blue T-shirt from the duffel with "GISS" printed on the shirt's chest in white letters. For no reason, he stuffed the clothing he had worn on the air that night into the duffel bag before returning it to the closet. Newly attired, he set up his phone camera to record every two hours for two minutes, starting eighteen minutes from the current time; it was 9:02 P.M. He extended a charger cable to the phone, noticing that it was still vibrating almost constantly with newly arriving texts. He set the phone to airplane mode and ignored the messages, even as he compiled a mental list of those most likely to have reached out. The list included a lot of unknowns, but one name was sure: Windsor.

Windsor would not have liked what happened tonight, and he would like what was about to happen even less. Jones wondered briefly what the puppet master would do when one of his most essential puppets deserted him.

With the office's blinds closed, he pulled the fans from their boxes, plugged them in, turned them all on at the low setting, and then arrayed them to face the seat where he would spend his last moments, two on the floor and one on the desk. He returned to the thermostat and saw another morsel of good news on this miraculous day: The temperature was down to 61. With the other zones in the large, empty building requiring no cooling, the spacious roof-top HVAC unit had an easy time bringing the temperature in the room down. He felt a pinch of thirst in the corner of his mouth and realized he was dehydrated from the stress of the evening and never drinking water in the studio. It was lucky; it meant that hypothermia could attack him sooner than if he were well-hydrated. While he seldom consumed alcohol, least of all alone, he remembered a bottle of wine someone had given him a year before. Drinking it would worsen the dehydration; even better, the direct effects of the alcohol on his system would help the hypothermia claim him sooner.

He looked at his watch—9:15 P.M., five minutes until the initial check-in. He wouldn't be around to edit the video and had no time to write code now to edit it in his absence, but he was certain that someone would somehow get the record of his last hours out to the public. Wasn't that how these things worked? He rechecked the thermostat and saw that the office temperature was down to 59 degrees. Next, he found the corkscrew in his desk drawer that the friend had included with the gift. He opened the bottle of red (somewhat expensive, if he were to guess) clumsily enough that he was glad not to have a witness, poured about a third of the ruby-red liquid into his office coffee mug, and drank it down. A minute later, at 9:16, he sat on the chair he had positioned for the shoot, felt the warmth from the wine suffuse his torso and soften his thoughts, and took a deep breath. *Were people always this happy when they were taking their own lives?* It didn't matter either way. He was experiencing one of the most fantastic nights of his life.

He tried to keep his breathing regular as the time approached for the initial video check-in and saw his phone's screen flicker to life as the camera app began recording. The words came to him effortlessly.

"My name is Nigel Jones. I am the head of climatology at NASA's Goddard Institute for Space Studies. I am also the next Fifty-Niner. My current body temperature"—he paused and inserted the thermometer sensor in his ear, read it, and then showed it to the camera—"as you can see is ninety-eight-point-nine degrees Fahrenheit. It was wrong of those of us who convinced the world's population that something terrible and unprecedented was happening with the climate. In a more normal era, that would have gone down as a footnote in an academic textbook. But in our time, one which I helped give rise to, our actions affected millions of mostly elderly, mostly solitary, and always vulnerable and impoverished human beings. When we created hysteria, we created fuel poverty, even if it wasn't our intention. And unfortunately, fuel poverty, in many cases, is lethal.

"I've arranged this video in a short time. Because of that, there is no readout on-screen of the ambient temperature in my office here at the institute." With this, he approached the phone, unplugged it from the charger, and walked it to the thermostat. "Nonetheless, as you can see"—with this, he focused the lens on the front of the thermostat—"the temperature in my office is fifty-nine degrees Fahrenheit. That will not change during the process that is unfolding." With this, he headed back to where he had propped up the phone, briefly focusing his camera lens on the fans along the way. "The temperature in this space and these fans, as was true with the other Fifty-Niners' endings, approximate the average conditions on our planet. These average phenomena that we human beings live in will now kill me. I have had a good life and attempted to do good. While I have failed, I hope I may undo some of the damage by giving my body to science, as it were. Remember the good times, Mum. I'm not doing anything tonight a good Samaritan wouldn't do to save people, no matter what it looks like."

30

For Whit, leaving the studio in the way he did had been a strategic decision that would define the public perception of him for now. He had become aware of Windsor's dominant, hidden role in all things climate on a plane trip to a conference in Singapore in 2015. It had happened after being bumped from a United Airlines flight from San Francisco, where he had been attending a pre-conference meeting with colleagues. He then managed to talk his way into a seat on a Singapore Airlines flight that would get him to his destination sooner. It turned out that people liked the airline for a reason. For the first time since he was a young boy flying with his parents, the romance of air travel was present to him. He even had a charming neighbor in the seat next to his reclining business-class seat, the neighbor being a polished and pretty blue-eyed political scientist headed to the same conference. He still felt uncomfortable, and always would, with the non-scientists attending climate conferences, but this woman had an undergraduate basis in hard science. It turned out she was also the niece of a man named James Windsor. When she heard that Whit's specialty was an ice-related climate science, she presumed it impossible he could hold views different from her own (and her uncle's) regarding climate. Making red wine disappear at a good clip, she laid out for Whit the connections her uncle possessed and the ways he had been leading from behind on climate for decades. Whit, no gifted actor, made it his mission not to let on that he was storing away everything the woman said, which he was.

He had an idea that what she shared with him would be useful tonight. On the flight, everything had become clear to him at once. Scientists, he reckoned, bore ten or fifteen percent of the responsibility for public hysteria about climate. Politicians could be blamed for another five or ten percent. But the gullible, Windsor-puppeted world media, guided to terrifying projections about climate like starving rats to cheese, were responsible for most public misconceptions about what was happening to their planet. Storms weren't the worst they had ever been. Droughts weren't the worst they had ever been. Sea level was slowly rising, as it had for thousands of years. Temperatures were not the warmest they had ever been. Not a single one of the supposed worst-ever conditions was indeed the worst ever. But none of that mattered. Windsor said it was the worst ever, with the way he pulled his puppeteer's strings, and so it *was* the worst ever.

Whit was sure that a man who wielded so much power would not give it up lightly, if at all. From the elevator bank at the bottom of 30 Rock, he half-jogged to a spot in front of Radio City Music Hall and hailed a yellow taxi.

"Where to?" the middle-aged, salt-and-pepper bearded driver asked him in what sounded like a Russian accent.

"Columbia campus," Whit said.

"One sixteen and Broadway," the driver said, pushing the button on his meter and pulling from the curb.

"That'll be fine," Whit said. "Actually . . . a hundred and twelfth and Broadway, northeast corner, please."

"One twelve and Broadway," the driver said. "You go to Tom's?" he asked, glancing in the rear-view mirror into Whit's eyes.

"Yup," Whit said. He had a hunch that spending time at the world-famous diner would allow him to verify.

"My cousin work there," the driver said.

"It's a good place," Whit said. He had spent a month on the Columbia campus during graduate school and the occasional week in the neighborhood visiting family before that. Tom's was a Greek-owned diner that served a few Greek specialties but mostly standard American diner fare. The milkshakes were over-priced—and excellent. His mouth watered thinking about the one he would order: vanilla ice cream and chocolate syrup, known as a "black-and-white shake" where he grew up.

"Better place to eat than work," the driver said.

"I've heard that," Whit said, partly to make conversation but also because it was something people used to say about every restaurant. He needed to do a few things that required his attention. "I've got to spend some time on the phone," he said.

"Iss okay," the driver said, "understand."

Whit had taken his phone off airplane mode in the elevator; only now did he see how many people had been trying to contact him. He saw messages from people on his side of the climate divide (all of whom he hoped would desist from becoming Fifty-Niners), plenty from numbers he didn't recognize, and one from Amy: "you got this, bro."

He wasn't sure he did have this, but he appreciated the encouragement. He thumbed a quick response—"maybe"—and put the phone in his pocket. He grabbed his battered, blue Mariners baseball hat, pulled it low on his head, then watched the foot traffic for the last several blocks of the trip until the taxi stopped in front of Tom's. He paid and generously tipped the driver with cash, who said, "zank you, have good night." He found a table near the back of the restaurant and took a seat facing 112th Street. He ordered his black-and-white milkshake and an order of French fries. It wasn't a typical night of eating for him, not at his age, but then again, it wasn't a standard night for him on any other level. The order took a long time, one thing that had not changed in so many years. He was glad the service was still slow; it allowed him to gather his thoughts and work up a better appetite. He also had texts to send, first to his cousin Irwin.

Irwin had gotten the same chances that Whit had when it came to receiving any education he might want, and he had chosen to study the law. Specifically, he had become a criminal defense attorney, a successful one. The career choice made sense; when they were younger, Irwin had committed crimes that needed defending, most drug-related and none serious. Along the way, the lawyers his family hired to keep him out of prison (and from having a criminal record) had become his heroes. Before ever committing actual crimes, though, he was doing things he shouldn't. It was the case almost every time Whit visited when they were young, and Whit had gotten him out of several scrapes that would have proved costly within the family. Whit had thus been there for Irwin at crucial junctures, and while he had planned never to call in the debt his cousin owed him, that plan had shifted during the ride uptown.

He knew that Irwin still had some odd habits. More importantly, he knew that Irwin still had close contacts throughout the Columbia University community, including, strangely enough, the undergraduate community. Sitting alone with his eyes scanning the sidewalk for Jones, whom he was pretty sure he would see letting himself into the institute any moment, Whit sent Irwin the first text in an exchange he knew would get his cousin's blood rushing.

WHIT: you home?

IRWIN: yeah, why?

WHIT: I'm probably going to need electronic access to the front door at McBain as well as a crowbar

IRWIN: where are you?

WHIT: I'm at Tom's

IRWIN: wtf, I'll be right there

WHIT: don't come here … I'll let you know when it's for sure I need the stuff

IRWIN: this is NOT like you

WHIT: you owe me

IRWIN: you don't have to tell me … I've got you

WHIT: sorry

IRWIN: anything else?

WHIT: yeah, you're going to need one of your friends to disable another Columbia building's alarm system remotely in about an hour

IRWIN: I could get in trouble for that, and so could you

WHIT: no getting around it, sorry

IRWIN: tell me when it's a sure thing

WHIT: will do

"One milkshake with vanilla ice cream and chocolate sauce, one order of fries," the waitress, a woman about his age with a faint Greek accent, said, putting his order in front of him. "Anything else?"

"No, thank you—just the check," Whit said, smiling politely.

"Pay the cashier," the woman said, leaving the check face-down on the table.

He took a sip of milkshake, separated a few fries from the pile in their oval bowl, and put them on a napkin to cool. After more sips of milkshake, he picked up a fry and carefully blew on it.

He paused for a two-count, then took a bite. It was perfect, still hot, but not enough to burn. The next sip of cold, sweet milkshake was made transcendent by the salt of the fry. The menu was overpriced, but they got the simple things right. Looking out the window, he saw a man awkwardly carrying fan boxes and a Duane Reade bag heading east on 112th Street.

It was one thing to have a hunch about what Jones would be doing on this night, but it was another to see him in the flesh during what Jones thought was a personal mission to get his scientific and personal karma right in one fell swoop. Whit felt a tug in his stomach as though someone dear to him was in peril. He wasn't surprised by the existence of the feeling, but he was surprised by its depth. He picked up his phone and texted Irwin.

WHIT: it's on

IRWIN: McBain access and a crowbar—what building are we knocking out the alarm of? Armstrong, presumably?

WHIT: good guess

IRWIN: I heard you had a couple of issues with them

WHIT: not a good time to be funny

IRWIN: no worries, where am I bringing the crowbar?

WHIT: I'll drop by your building reception; there in six minutes

Irwin had schemed his way into a Columbia apartment on Riverside, just west of Barnard campus. It was against policy for anyone not actively affiliated with the university to lease any Columbia apartment, but he had managed. It had something to do with his second wife, a law professor. Before she died of a gruesome form of cancer, she had tied keeping the lease in his name to a gift from her family to the law school. So far as Whit had known, the wife hadn't liked Irwin all that much, but he supposed actions spoke more than loudly than words. Whit paid and zig-zagged to Irwin's, moving north and west according to whichever light was green.

His cousin was sitting on granite masonry next to a stone, circular planter in front of his building when Whit first spied him. As Whit drew near, Irwin stood and came in for a hug, a vape pen in one hand and a tennis racket bag, presumably holding the crowbar, in the other.

"Good night for tennis," Whit said, "thank you."

"It's always a good night for tennis," Irwin said, "I've been telling you for years." Irwin, red-haired and freckle-faced no less than he had been when they were young, shared Whit's athletic presence. He sported a trench coat and thick black glasses, both of which would have made good disguising choices. The truth was, though, they were just his look, more or less unchanged since college. Behind Irwin's glasses his pale blue, quizzical eyes looked at Whit with warmth.

"This will be my only night, but thank you again," Whit said, taking the racket bag.

"Here's an active Columbia faculty ID with your photo," Irwin said, handing the card to Whit.

"You work fast," Whit said.

"Easy-peasy," Irwin said. "Look at it." Whit held the card a few inches from his face and saw that it was a standard Columbia faculty card, perfectly accomplished and with a plausible name he barely took in, with his photo from the University of Colorado staring back at him.

"Wow," Whit said. "I don't even want to know how this is possible."

"What time do you want the alarm off in Armstrong?" Irwin said, drawing on his vape pen and blowing out a vapor cloud.

"Those aren't much less disgusting than cigarettes, but I'm told they kill you less reliably," Whit said. "As soon as you can on the alarm; you have no idea how helpful this is."

"I guess I don't," Irwin said. "I could have gotten you in the front door of Armstrong, but you don't want that, I assume."

"I need to be as invisible as I can moving forward tonight," Whit said. "That's why I thought to make my way in indirectly."

"I'm sure it makes sense in some universe," Irwin said. "Great seeing you again; it's only been fifteen years."

"I know," Whit said, pulling his cousin in for a quick bear hug and then striding away.

31

Whit was walking uptown, not because he had business in that direction but to get out of his cousin's sight. He also didn't want anyone but Irwin to have any idea of what he was doing next. At 120th Street, he turned right, walking the shortened block before crossing Claremont Avenue, then shooting a text to the NBC woman. "Hey Erica, it's Whit Thorgason," he texted. Before he could contemplate continuing toward Broadway, she responded: "where are you?" Figuring that their back-and-forth would require a couple of minutes, he leaned his carry-on bag and the loaned tennis bag against a building, rested his back against the building's cool stone wall, and started texting.

WHIT: had someone to see

ERICA: apparently

WHIT: sorry ... abrupt, I know

ERICA: where are you?

WHIT: uptown ... sorry to ask but need help with something

ERICA: you probably ended my career tonight ... wasn't that enough?

WHIT: I doubt that; I know it didn't look good for a minute

ERICA: what could I possibly do for you?

WHIT: I need any phone numbers you have for James Windsor

ERICA: I might have ONE for him

WHIT: he's in tight with you people; you must have two or three
ERICA: 917-555-8717
WHIT: thank you ... have other(s)?
ERICA: 917-555-2344 ... 917-555-6393 ...
WHIT: is one the best, any idea?
ERICA: the last one ... you got none from me
WHIT: sorry to be in a rush; thank you
ERICA: good luck

He knew how unusual it was for anyone in her shoes to help someone on his side; the fact that Erica had shown courage twice to assist him was moving. But it was no time to get choked up; there was much to do.

WINDSOR'S TEAM had produced several communications in the first hour after the debate ended, including a statement on behalf of Jones, though no one could currently get ahold of him. The old man was incensed by the radio silence even more than he was by the scientist's breakdown and on-air admission. The more he thought about it, the more wrathful he became. All employees had been multi-tasked, over-tasked if he was honest about it, and they had left him to try to gain control over himself in his office. The communications superstructure that he had constructed over forty years was at risk of being brought down by a single scientist publicly losing his mind. Repairing the damaged bits would be exhausting, expensive, and, worst of all, humiliating. The last fact was making the bottom of his thoughts fall dangerously away from him. His business would endure; that was a sure thing, but he was less certain of his own mind and even his own living body.

Windsor had paid for an expensive coating on his tall office windows, making it impossible for anyone to see in, day or night. He had nonetheless closed his cream-colored drapes to practice an art he'd mastered as a boy that required privacy. He had even put on a gray sweatsuit for the occasion, which, combined with the gray hair on his head, made him look even older than he was.

It was simple, and he suspected that there were other practitioners around the world. It consisted of striking the side of his head with the heels of his hands, right then left, with great force. His parents never laid a hand on him as he grew up, for which he never forgave them. For his most recent seventy years, though, he had made up for their dereliction of duty. Tonight, the blows came with great intensity. They hurt his hands in addition to his head: right-left, right-left, right-left, and so on. It was heavenly. An extraordinary clarity always emerged, sometimes in as few as four strikes. The Zen quiet was undeniable after ten blows tonight, but he kept going for five minutes, losing track of how many times he'd struck his head. No matter: he was healed, breathing well again. He knew that tonight was not his failure or anyone else's. It merely was. Rectifying the situation would be entertaining if he only allowed it to be.

His phone vibrated on his desk, giving his heart a jolt of happiness. Whoever the call was from, it would be the bridge that carried him back to safety so that he could continue rescuing the world from the greatest scourge it had known, humankind. The call was a request to FaceTime from someone with a Boulder area code. He pressed ACCEPT and was unsurprised to see the face of Whit Thorgason—outdoors, on what looked like the Upper West Side. The yellow streetlight glow on Thorgason's face made him look a little like a space alien.

"Good evening!" Whit said.

"I wouldn't go that far," Windsor said.

"You're not going to be able to get in touch with Jones," Whit said.

"Dr. Thorgason? Or should I call you *Whit*, you contemptible prick?" Windsor said.

"I'd be upset, too. I get it," Whit said.

"If you think losing your career is the worst thing that can happen to a man, you are mistaken," Windsor said. "But, then, you've been mistaken all your life."

"I guess I'll tell Jones you're not interested in communicating with him," Whit said.

"You will do no such thing," Windsor said.

"It's funny you have such a strong opinion about what he should or shouldn't hear when you have no way of getting in touch with him yourself," Whit said.

"My staff will have him in my office within an hour," Windsor said. "You can bank on it."

"Guess who the next Fifty-Niner is going to be?" Whit said. "I'll give you a hint. It's not me. Any guesses?"

"You're out of your mind," Windsor said. "He's crazy, but not like you."

"He's not crazy at all," Whit said. "He's a good man who is finally redeeming himself."

"You're lying," Windsor said.

"You're smarter than that," Whit said. "You know the ring of truth when you hear it; I am not making this up."

"He's not going to do that, I'm confident of that, but—" Windsor said.

"But—?" Whit said.

"But if he did, it would be the best thing that ever happened to him, and the best thing he ever did for science," Windsor said.

"I always knew you had your dark side, but ... wow," Whit said.

"Go 'wow' yourself," Windsor said.

"Let me know if you want to talk to Jones," Whit said. "Ciao for now."

When the screen on Windsor's phone went dark, it occurred to him he might have hit himself one too many times. He wasn't feeling well, and the clarity he'd found during the self-flagellation was just a hazy memory. He walked to a reclining chair he had never used since buying it in 2006, contemplated sitting in it now, then flipped the chair over in a rage.

WHIT PRESSED END; the video connection disappeared. He had needed to give Windsor the impression that he was looking for a reward for putting him in touch with Jones.

He checked his watch: 10:52 P.M. His phone was blowing up with new messages on a near-constant basis. One of the most recent ones was one from Erica Nagle: "call me ... please."

He pushed a button and brought the phone to his ear, barely registering that he was still on Claremont Avenue. It was a weird spot to spend more than a minute or two.

"Thank you," Erica said.

"No sweat," Whit said, "something up?"

"You could say that," she said.

"Did you want me to guess?" Whit said.

"Sorry, my mind is racing," she said. "Most of the most famous climate scientists in the world, even ones who haven't tweeted before, are tweeting about Jones."

"That doesn't surprise me," Whit said.

"No?"

"Not a bit; it's Windsor's people."

"It's not press releases we're seeing; they're tweets," Erica said.

"I know, I get it," Whit said. "I'd bet my pinkie toe that Windsor's team controls their Twitter accounts, or at least has access. That's how this has been going down for a long time. The scientists can tweet, themselves, here and there, but they feel like tight-rope walkers when they communicate for themselves, and they mostly leave it to the pros."

"Can you prove that?" Erica asked.

"I don't need to prove it; I'm telling you."

"That doesn't help much," she said. "Your side is not coming off well. MSNBC is posting tweets every few minutes, and each is worse than the last. *The Today Show* tomorrow will be a shit show for you guys. It's probably the end unless you can think of something."

"Thanks for the heads-up," Whit said.

"That's it?"

"The night is young," he said, pushing END.

A message from Erica came three seconds later. It contained a screenshot of a tweet from an astrophysicist who had added climatology to his résumé mid-career, as though it were a knick-knack one bought on vacation. But he was perceived as a thoughtful world-saver who could do no wrong.

"@NigelJones, like many brilliant human beings, depends on anti-psychotic medication that he hates to take ... tonight we saw the true strain climatologists live with ... #prayforNigel"

Whit messaged Erica back: "Nigel wins."

Erica's response was: "?"

Whit texted: "He wins, I promise, gotta run."

Whit had the tools he needed to get into McBain, the building he planned to use as his stepping-stone into Armstrong. He had initially wanted Jones to spend sufficient time in 59-degree conditions, with a trio of fans speeding his seeming demise, for the experience to make an impression on him. He knew that the longer Jones believed he was a Fifty-Niner, the greater would be his reluctance to give up on being one, but also the more the experience would help to restore his sense of self.

But giving him extra time alone in the cold with his last thoughts was turning into a dangerous luxury, Whit realized. He did not know Windsor was on a rampage in his midtown office. Still, he did know that Windsor Communications was generating a tidal wave of lies that showed how serious the company, and by extension, everyone associated with it was taking the debate. Whit figured that if Windsor hadn't dispatched employees to track down Jones to bring him into his office, it was only a matter of time before he did. Whit figured he might only have half an hour to locate Jones in a large building and talk him out of wasting his considerable talents. The Fifty-Niners had already had whatever success they could reasonably expect. Whit knew he needed to move on to the next battle over the fate of science and, therefore, of humankind. As for the rest of the evening, it was time to save Jones from his awakened conscience.

In the end, Whit chose not to cross Claremont. Instead, he took his bags in his hands and walked at top speed downtown, sticking to the west side of the tiny avenue until it terminated at 116th Street. He waited for a yellow cab to pass, looked both ways, and made his way across the crosswalk to the south side of 116th Street, turning left (and east) toward Broadway. Again, he speed-walked to the southwest corner of 112th Street and Broadway to afford himself the best view of Armstrong and the Goddard Institute for Space Studies. He'd hoped to see Jones's office from where he now stood, sweating and a bit out of breath.

There had been the sense on his way that someone might be following him, which was not a typical thought for him. It also didn't make any sense. He told himself to breathe and to settle down and then raised his eyes, finally, to search the upper floors of Armstrong's façade. Sure enough, on the sixth floor, the only light in the building, muted by blinds, was in a corner office. There was one, and only one, occupied office facing Broadway or 112th Street. It had to be Jones.

Whit pushed the button to cross and waited for the signal. As he stepped into the crosswalk, he felt a firm hand on his right shoulder and heard a deep, muffled voice: "Mr. Thorgason, we're going to need you to come with us." He wheeled, ready for whatever awaited. Then saw that the voice had come from Irwin, who had perpetrated any number of practical jokes over the years using a gift to produce voices other than his own convincingly.

"Not good, Irwin," Whit said. "I have no time, and you know that."

"You're going to need protection," Irwin said, gesturing with his eyes to a knot of serious-looking men over his shoulder. They had military haircuts, wore dark clothing, and smoked as though it were excellent for their health. There were six of them, and Whit saw upon closer analysis that they had Secret Service-style earpieces. When he returned his glance to Irwin, he saw that Irwin had one himself.

"Say something to them," Whit said.

"Guys, everybody look up for a second," Irwin said.

Six heads looked up and then back down. The men exchanged darkly amused looks and kept on smoking.

"Jesus, Irwin," Whit said.

"You're in deeper than you know," Irwin said. "That's hard for a hero to hear, but it was always true."

"God damn it, Irwin. I'm serious. I don't have time for this. I appreciate the gesture, but—"

"It's not negotiable," Irwin said.

Breaking into a national science facility was a risky enough endeavor; breaking into it with Eastern European mafia thugs, or whoever Irwin's associates were, was madness. He wouldn't do it. He couldn't, even if he half-wanted to, which he didn't.

"Your friends can guard the roof and the elevator entrances on the first and sixth floors. That's my compromise. The guy I need to chat with is in that office," Whit said, nodding toward Jones's muted office light near the top of Armstrong. "None of your guys are in the room with me, including you."

"Thank God," Irwin said. "Being bored to death has always been one of my deepest fears."

He gave his cousin a look Whit remembered from childhood, a combination of affection and sarcasm only Irwin could produce.

"Do you need to tell them anything?" Whit said, glancing toward Irwin's team.

"Nope," Irwin said. "They follow me like puppy dogs." It was a scary thought.

"I'm not in love with the idea of the eight of us walking through the front door of a dorm together," Whit said. "I can think of subtler entrances."

"Guys," Irwin said. "You're going to need to find your own way in." One particularly serious-looking team member gave a faint look of recognition regarding Irwin's order on behalf of them all.

"That's it?" Whit asked.

"That's it," Irwin said.

"Okay, it's now," Whit said. "Catch up with you at the next family reunion."

"Good seeing you," Irwin said. He looked as happy as when they were fifteen years old, two kids goofing on the shores of Lake Washington in the summertime before the ax had fallen on Whit's parents' careers as practicing scientists.

"Yeah," Whit said. The family never held reunions. Irwin inserting himself into this episode in his life was not something he anticipated being able to forgive.

He again pushed the crossing button but saw the letters had turned white for a woman on the other side of the street who was crossing toward him. Whit looked down as they passed, using the bill of his Mariners cap as a shield. He turned left in front of Tom's, keeping his chin down and walking with long strides. Irwin and his team were behind, around, or ahead of him. There was no way to know without craning his neck all around, and even if he did, he was unlikely to be able to identify them. They were men who could disappear when the need arose. At 113th Street, he turned right. He pulled out the ID card Irwin had given him, flashed it at the sensor, and let himself in after hearing the lock's click. He looked around the small lobby and saw what he learned was an unalarmed door on his right. The metal knob turned quickly in his hand, and he let himself in and waited for the door to close before starting up the seven flights of stairs.

He took them two by two, using legs strengthened by years of climbing glaciers for work and ascending mountains for fun. His thoughts centered on the last request he had sent Erica and how Irwin's crew would make their way into Armstrong, which he still felt to be an excessive show of force. He'd sent a text to Erica from the corner of 120th Street and Claremont: "wait for me, not alone, outside Goddard Institute for Space Studies at 112th and B'way starting at midnight . . . and if you can have a large camera from work there that would be good . . . thank you." He thought she would probably be where he'd asked when the time came, but he couldn't be sure. As for Irwin's goon squad, he had no idea.

He had made it to the landing that included a door to the roof; he saw the predictable fire-alarm-armored handle. From his experience, this could be a serious problem—or no problem at all. He liked spending time on rooftops and had made his way to a few dozen of them, on various university campuses, over the years. Sometimes a fire alarm on an emergency exit door was functional, but often it wasn't. It tended to be a rude shock when you tested one, and it turned out to be live. When they were functioning, the circuits they ran on were separate from a building's primary system, so it hadn't been something Irwin could have handled remotely. In Whit's experience, the more prestigious the university, the less likely its fire alarms would be functional. Even though Columbia was on the prestigious side, he hated to take the risk. He contemplated texting Irwin to have one of his team members come to take care of it (which Whit was confident they were each capable of) but decided against it. Irwin was already more involved than Whit would have chosen; asking for help a second time was inviting annoyance, at a minimum, if not disaster. And something told him he needed to hurry. Even if he did make the request, it would take time.

He placed a hand on the push bar and gave a shove. The door opened, and no alarm came. The cool night air hit his cheeks; he took a breath and let himself out. He and Irwin had gotten onto more than one Columbia rooftop as teenagers during summer visits that alternated between the East Coast and the West Coast, Irwin having grown up in an apartment on Riverside a few blocks from campus. Though pressed for time, Whit allowed himself to enjoy the 360-degree view of the Upper West Side, including nearby Riverside Park and the dark ribbon of the Hudson River, for a single moment, then walked to the edge of the building. He would need to drop about eleven feet to Armstrong's roof. Leaning as far as he safely could from McBain, he dropped first the tennis bag, then his suitcase, using its extendable handle to lessen the distance and the tennis bag to soften the traveling bag's impact. He hung by his hands before dropping to the black-tar roof and landing safely. He briefly worried that any sounds had been audible to Jones but dismissed the thought; he was on the other side of the building and one floor down. These buildings were thick-walled; it was unlikely he would have heard a thing.

Whit opened the tennis bag and removed the crowbar. Then he picked up both bags and walked to the roof door leading to the stairwell. He had less experience jimmying doors than Irwin, he was sure, but despite a stab of doubt that came while sliding the end of the crowbar between door and frame, he got the thing open with minimum effort. Or he was so hopped up on adrenalin that it just had made it seem easy. Regardless, he hadn't damaged the door too much for it to shut, which it did behind him. He might need the crowbar again to get into the sixth floor from the stairs, which he took in a flutter. Like the first one, the door was steel and windowless. Although tempted to insert the crowbar and have at it, he took the fraction of a second required to reach out and try the round steel handle. It caught at first and then turned easily in his hand. Once through, he saw the light on the other side of a bullpen of cubicles coming through Jones's Venetian blinds. Whit paused to put the crowbar in the tennis bag and gather his thoughts for a conversation that promised to be complicated.

Standing on the gray carpet outside Jones's office, he took a long breath and reached for yet another door handle.

32

Jones's door seemed the most likely of all those Whit had tried to be locked. When its handle turned in his hand, he experienced a moment of surprise that verged on fear. Before he could think about it, though, he found himself accosted by an embarrassed and angry Jones, who wore gym clothes and had been sitting with fans pointed at him and now was on his feet coming toward Whit with strange menace. Once he understood who had come to his office, Jones went to sit in front of the fans again.

"Give me this," Jones said to Whit.

"You got caught in another man's game," Whit said.

"Yeah, yours," Jones said, "and now you're trying to change the rules."

"There are no rules," Whit said. "And I recognize the humanity in what you are doing—and the courage. You do not have to prove that you are a good man. I know you are a good man, and you know it. That should be enough."

"I've caused damage," Jones said.

"You have," Whit said. "I have. It's human to cause damage. It's also human to do something about it. But this will not fix anything."

"No?" Jones said. Whit saw, for the first time, that Jones's lips were blue. He had only been at it for two and a half hours, and he looked colder than he should have.

"Why do you look so cold?" Whit asked.

"I take blood thinners," Jones said. "I had a pulmonary embolism a few years back, and they put me on them then. I'm always cold. I was sort of pleased about how easy it would make tonight."

"Studies say they don't make you colder than people not on them, but—" Whit said.

"But they do," Jones said.

"I know," Whit said. "My mom's been on them for decades. It changed what she could do on glaciers. She was devastated. What is your temperature?"

"I did a video half an hour ago," Jones said. "It was 97.5 degrees."

"That's cold enough to feel bad or maybe even aggressive," Whit said, with a hint of a smile.

"You think?" Jones said, lifting a gooseflesh-covered arm for Whit to observe.

"Are you shaking yet?" Whit said.

"A little bit," Jones said. "Trying not to. What were you talking about when you said, 'someone else's game'?"

"I'm sure you've thought about it," Whit said.

"I've thought about a lot for the past few hours," Jones said, "and I don't know who you mean. Not with certainty."

"Windsor," Whit said.

"Go on," Jones said.

"I'm surprised he's not here," Whit said. "I'd bet a good amount he's on his way."

"To stop me?" Jones said. "Why would you tell him what I was doing?"

"Because I wanted to show you this," Whit said, holding up his phone and pushing play on a video screen grab he had made of the call with Windsor. "Watch until the end," he said.

Jones took the phone and watched with it in his hands, which were shaking. After seeing the whole thing, he rewound and listened to the end again, raising the volume to maximum.

"But if he did," Windsor's voice intoned, "it would be the best thing that ever happened to him and the best thing he ever did for science."

"So why would he come here if he's so excited about my doing this thing for science?" Jones said. His eyes looked like they did at the debate just before his first tears.

"He said your suicide would be good for science out of anger, but he knows it would be hard for him and the rest of his ilk to explain," Whit said. "You and some other well-intentioned and brilliant people got used by Windsor and others like him. But he's the best of the best."

The door opened, and Windsor stepped into the room flanked by five men in business suits with earpieces like the ones on Irwin's men. Windsor was in a burgundy mock turtleneck, faded jeans, and the same cowboy boots he came to New York wearing decades before; his face bore an apprising snarl.

"I'm sure he just played you the tape of his and my conversation," Windsor said. His enforcers formed a semi-circle behind him. They looked highly focused, if less intimidating than Irwin's crew had.

You couldn't see their weapons, but there was no doubt each of them had one. "If volcano man did show it to you," Windsor said, "I'm sure your feelings are a little hurt. That was not my intention. I had my reasons for speaking the words I did, but they did not represent my actual thoughts about you. You are a valuable and brilliant scientist, and you will need to come with us to make right what happened at the debate tonight, as the better angel of your nature would have it."

"You've got to be kidding," Jones said.

"He's not," Whit said. "I didn't know PR people hired thugs, Windsor. Who are your friends?"

"These men are Department of Defense policemen," Windsor said. "Badges, gentlemen!" All five flashed Department of Defense badges and pocketed them.

"Wow," Whit said. "Don't move, Dr. Jones. You don't want to go with these guys. Windsor would need a very high security clearance to have DoD police at his disposal, and when he said what he said on the video to me, it was exactly how he feels about you and anyone who dares stand in his way. He's a thug."

"*I'm* a thug?" Windsor said. He took a step toward Whit as though he wanted to do violence personally.

"How'd you get in here?" Jones said. He was still sitting in front of the fans, nurturing the hope of fulfilling his evening's ambition, despite everything happening in front of him.

"I've had keys and a security card to this rat trap for a long time," Windsor said. "I never liked it here, but access has proved useful now and again."

The door burst open, and before the members of Windsor's security team could draw weapons, Irwin's men, guns in hand, had stepped into the office, with Irwin coming through the door last.

"Party!" Irwin said.

"These men are United States Department of Defense police officers," Windsor said, "and you will drop your weapons on the floor."

"I love this guy," Irwin said, "definitely a movie fan! Here's the deal, I want you to look in the eyes of your DoD friends, and then I want you to look in the eyes of *my* colleagues. And then I want you to shut your fucking mouth until I tell you otherwise. As for you, DoD dudes, this is not personal. Put your hands behind your backs, and these gentlemen will gently zip-tie them for your safety."

To the surprise of only Windsor, the DoD police did as they were told. Not one had ever been involved in an armed standoff. Irwin's crew, conversely, had been through a few dozen each. They *liked* them.

Whit stepped to a spot near Windsor and looked down at the suddenly cowed PR wizard, who until then had fancied himself one of the most powerful men in the country, with reason.

"You don't want people to hear about tonight," Whit said, "and you especially don't want them hearing that you brought these guys here to kidnap a scientist who dared to disagree with you. When I leave here, I'm going to see that a copy of our video chat gets into the hands of a major-network news producer waiting outside. She will broadcast it, ending your little run as the rodent who ruled the earth for a time. I also videoed everything that just happened in this room. If you do anything to threaten the well-being or independence of myself, Dr. Jones, or anyone else in the room, then the second video will go to the producer, and you will spend some of your last years of life behind bars. Do you understand?"

Windsor looked at him blankly.

"Nod yes," Whit said.

Windsor nodded.

"Attaboy," Whit said. "Dr. Jones, would you like to be the one to zip-tie this reptile's scaly wrists together?"

"I'll pass," Jones said.

"Wrists behind, please," Whit said, zip-tying Windsor's wrists and sitting him on the floor next to his enforcers. "Dr. Jones, it's been a night. What do you say we get you back in street clothes and start planning some research projects? Sound good?"

"I want to measure things," Jones said, standing and picking up the gym bag holding his street clothes from his desk.

"I know you do," Whit said. "All scientists like to measure things."

"That do it for tonight?" Irwin said.

Whit gave a hug that just about cracked his cousin's spine.

"I'll be in touch," Whit said.

"Sure, you will," Irwin said. "And I don't mind."

33

Climatism is not the kind of thing that ends with a bang. It is too well-funded and too entrenched for that ever to be the case.

But the night that Windsor brought his Department of Defense goons to the Goddard Institute for Space Studies to encourage a NASA climatologist to accompany him against his will out of the building did pull an important thread from the fabric of climate doomsaying. Windsor, though he continued to go into the office, never contacted NBC News again. And the communications that his shop produced about climate lost a little of their true-believer sheen. Everyone on his staff knew they had seen the high-water mark of Climatism and had been a part of it personally. It was something many of them mourned, but none more than the old man himself.

Sensing this small shift in the war between reason and Climatism, a crotchety Australian uranium-mining magnate, Maggie Pearson, funded the first truly independent climate-science program in the Western Hemisphere at the University of Alaska. It was the only program not built with piles of money originating in noble-cause corruption, and its first chair was a second-generation volcanologist with a penchant for wearing Seattle Mariners ball caps. In the weeks after the debate, Whit had begun an intensive mentorship of Jones on glacial volcanoes, in which Jones had a more than academic interest. He loved them with a purity that rivaled that of Whit himself. Fifteen months after the debate, Jones was studying in a fast-track PhD program that would culminate in three years.

One surprising addition to the community in Fairbanks was Juanita Tagawa. While Whit had been impressed by Jones's courage on the night that he tried to become a Fifty-Niner, Juanita was smitten. She booked a ticket to Denver and was waiting with Amy for Whit and Jones when they pulled up to the curb at Whit and Amy's house three days after the debate. Juanita spent the next week with Whit's family in Boulder and came to realize that it hadn't been equal parts Michael's handsomeness and courage that had drawn her to him. In fact, it had nearly all been his courage. In this new place, and in this unexpected new segment in her life, she showed Jones how she felt about his courage with glances and little gestures of affection. Jones, a lifelong loner, was reborn in the light of her intelligence, beauty, and warmth. Before the end of the visit, he was in love.

Having grown up in one of the world's great surfing nations, as New Zealand was, Jones had, strangely and improbably, never seen someone on a surfboard in his life, in person, let alone tried the sport. From his earliest memories, he was a nerd's nerd. Despite inhaling the knowledge of volcanoes Whit imparted to him, he was less apt when it came to learning to stand on a shifting board in a cascading torrent known as a wave. But in the end, drawing on guts that Juanita reminded him he possessed, he did ride a wave for the first time during his second summer at U. of A., in a remote cove on Kodiak Island. Covered in black neoprene from the top of his head to his hands and feet, he yelled in exultation as the wave sped him forward, loud enough for some of the local bears to hear. After that, he became a competent, if not world-class, surfer during other forays to the coast on seaplanes that Whit organized for his family and their new friends, as well as on jaunts to Chile with his beloved Juanita.

The two were married one week after he defended his dissertation. A proud Whit was one of his dissertation committee members, and when Jones gained a full-time position late that fall, Juanita was already expecting their first child. Jones was so much happier than he had ever been in his life that it never again occurred to him to change the historical record for a temperature station in the world. It was hard to believe—when he was honest about it—that he ever had, hard to believe that anyone had.

Amy was granted her own tenured position at the university, and she and Whit and their girls entered a time that they all would treasure. The girls found all the friends they could ever want. Spending every spare minute in nature, the family adopted two Alaskan huskies, one of whom they named Reykjavik. Every so often, Erica Nagle or another from the world of "news" reached out for comment on a story involving climate. Whit never said yes to anyone but Erica. The memory of his friends, the Fifty-Niners, haunted him. It was Juanita's idea that they hold an annual ceremony remembering all nineteen of their lives, lighting nineteen candles, and saying a few quiet words of gratitude. With candlelight flickering on the faces of those he held dear, Whit thanked his departed brothers for their sacrifice. Within hours or days, depending on how strongly the event affected him each year, he would return to doing his best to give people sufficient time to prepare for the next climate-altering volcanic eruption. It was always his fear that it would come soon.

*Bleak, dark, and piercing cold, it was a night for
the well-housed and fed to draw round the bright fire,
and thank God they were at home; and for the
homeless starving wretch to lay him down and die.*

—Charles Dickens, *Oliver Twist*

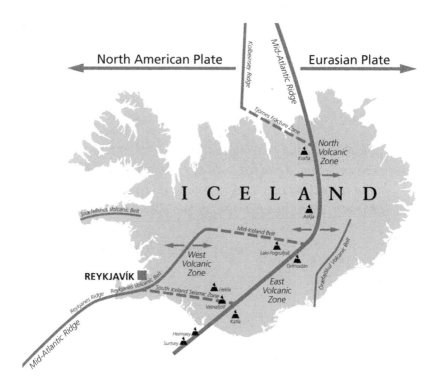

Illustration by Peter Hermes Furian

Made in United States
North Haven, CT
25 February 2023

33177646R00137